PUBLICATIONS PRESENTS

A novel by

AMANDA LEE

5 Star Publications
PO BOX 471570
Forestville, MD 20753

Deranged 2

ISBN -13: 978-0983247357
ISBN-10: 0983247358
Library of Congress Control Number: 2011915303
First Printing: May 2012

Printed in the United States

All stories are a work of fiction from the authors and are not meant to depict, portray, or represent any particular real person. Names, characters, places, and incidents are either the product of the author's imagination or are used fictitiously, and any resemblance to an actual person living or dead is entirely coincidental.

www.5starpublications.net
www.tljestore.com
www.facebook.com/authoramandalee

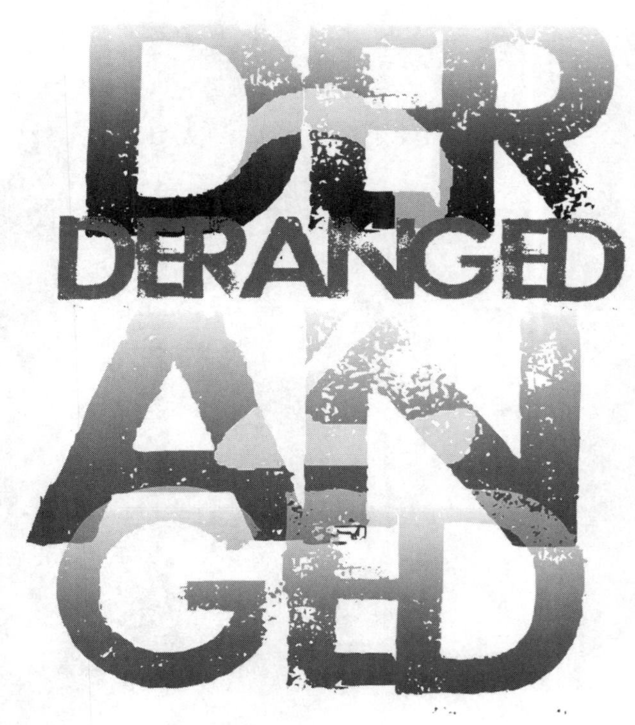

A novel by

AMANDA LEE

STAR

Prologue

Fuck. My eyes are barely open, and I'm sitting on this hard-ass floor, looking up at a bright light. My head is banging, and I hear people screaming. My vision is very blurry, and all I can see are people running around like chickens with their heads cut off. I hold my hands up. Blood is running down my fingers. I look up at the people running around and try to open my eyes more to focus, and I see a woman lying on the floor with blood oozing from her eyes. I wipe my eyes and look again. This bitch has both her eyeballs dug out of the sockets. All of these people are yelling at me. I look at my hands and look at the woman again. I shake my head slowly.

In a room of what appears to be a mental hospital, something on the floor catches my attention; I look over to see an eyeball staring back at me. I scream. I jump up and run until I hit a wall. My body falls helplessly to the floor and my eyes roll into the back of my head as people gather around me.

"Ma'am, are you alright?" I hear a male voice ask.

"Tie this crazy bitch up," another male voice instructs angrily. "We don't need any more problems than we already have. Get some ropes and tie her hands together, so she won't hurt anybody else."

"Fuck that! I'm giving her ass a shot. Then, we can tie her up. This bitch is crazy," a female voice angrily replies.

I look to my right just as the nurse shoves a needle deep into my arm and I feel the medicine pour deep into me. The nurse stands up. Then, she pulls out another needle.

The man says, "You can't give her two shots. It will kill her."

"Who gives a damn? She killed Bertha. Look at her," the nurse points over to the lady.

"Keep your voice down," the male replies.

The next thing I know, my eyes are closing. These muther-fuckers are trying to kill me. *Once I get out of this shit, I'm going to kill all these bitches. Believe that*, I think.

*****

Hours later, I open my eyes and try to focus. I look around and see only smoky gray walls. I turn my head to the left, as if in slow motion; then I turn my head to the right. I'm puzzled like a muther-fucker. As I look up and down, I notice that they have moved me to a different room. Fright causes me to sit straight up like a stiff board. I look around and try to find the blood and eyeballs on the floor that I had seen earlier. I jump up from the floor and run over to the door. I bang and bang on it, and then I stop abruptly. My head is hurting really bad. I touch my forehead, and I feel a huge knot, feels like I have been beaten. I turn around to face the back of the small-ass room and I think out loud as clicking noises invade my mind. *Click, click, click.*

*****

What the hell? I slipped up bad this time, Nicole thinks as she realizes her body has gone too far.

"Bitch, they got us," I say to Nicole.

"Nikki, you deserve to be put away. You are literally crazy," Nicole replies.

"You stupid-ass bitch, you're in here too, or did you somehow overlook that fact?" I yell.

"Shut up Nikki! I told you to stop being an out-of-control psychopath," Nicole replies to herself.

"Fuck you! We're in a fucking nut house. A loony bin! A crazy place! I'm not insane."

"You're crazy as fuck Nikki," Nicole says, sounding disgusted.

"Bitch, are you listening? You and I are locked up in this bitch together," I reply harshly.

"I can't believe you got us in here," Nicole responds.

"What the fuck? Why in the hell am I locked up with a dumb-ass like you? I didn't get us into this bullshit by myself. You got us into this shit, fucking off with Jeremy," I remind her.

"Shut up Nikki! I love Jeremy, and there is nothing you can do about it," Nicole says.

"There is plenty I can do, bitch. I can kill him, and then kill you. Don't think I haven't thought about getting rid of your weak ass. I need a down bitch, not a muther-fucker that cries like a baby," I sneer.

"You wouldn't dare kill him. We are together as one. And for you to think about killing me? Well, that lets me know you are no longer on my side. I thought we would be together forever," Nicole answers.

"We are together forever, but I'm taking over! Your weakness is causing me too many fucking problems. Look around, Nicole," I say to her. "We are locked up in a loony bin, and who knows for how fucking long," I continue as I pace the floor frantically.

"This is your fault, Nikki. You didn't have to kill, but you did," Nicole says as she points a finger in my face, while looking at me in the reflective window located in the door.

"Bitch, I killed for you, not me. I can't believe I'm protecting an ungrateful, dumb bitch," I say to Nicole as she stares back at me.

"Stop calling me a dumb bitch."

"I speak my mind, and you don't. If a chick is dumb, then a chick is dumb," I say to Nicole again.

"I love you Nikki, but you need to know one thing— I will take you out the game before I let you kill me," Nicole says harshly.

"Just try it. You will never live to see another day," I threaten.

I take my thoughts away from her as I pace back and forth, wondering what the hell I can do to break myself away from this nut case. My heart races, like when I first tried ecstasy, and I begin to sweat as tears form in my eyes. I slide down the wall, and I cry out loud. My body trembles, and I can't take it anymore. Here I am, laying on the floor like a broke down muther-fucker on crack. I cry and cry, praying that God will take away this pain I have in my heart. I have tried to forget all the hurt, but this shit is like a sore. Telling people I am hurting is not an option. Who can I really tell? My mother fucked me as a kid, while my father fucked both me and my sister. My grandparents aren't around to comfort me, and I have no brothers. My aunts love me, but their good intentions just always start trouble for me with my mother. I was just a child, but all this shit happened to me before I turned six. Muther-fuckers didn't care that I was a child though.

I look up at the ceiling, hoping I can get a sign for why all this happened.

"God, why me? I've always tried to be a good girl. I was hurt when I was a child, not as an adult. So, when will the pain ever go away? Help me, please help," I cry as I continue to look toward the ceiling.

I curl up into the fetal position and begin to bite myself very hard. The first thought to cross my mind is *Maybe, if I bite the main veins out of my arm, I will die and never have to experience pain again. This hurt Jeremy has placed upon my heart is unbearable.*

Then it dawns on me that if I kill myself, there will be no more loving Jeremy. Fuck that! I want to live the rest of my life with that nigga. I don't want to go through this life without him. I refuse to live without him. It still hurts me that he'd let these muther-fuckers cage me up like a fucking animal. I'm not an animal, and I damn sure am not crazy. Everybody wants to say that I got played by a nigga, and now, I can't handle rejection. That may be true, but he will regret his decision.

I continue to lie on the floor with my head to my knees. The tears won't stop running down my face. I must get a grip, but my heart won't let me. It aches and aches like I have been stabbed. Jeremy took all my hopes and dreams away. I know deep down, that he loves me. We have been through too much for him not to care about me. I care about this nigga so much that I'm willing to kill again for him.

I stop crying and sit up against the wall. I look around, observe my surroundings, and see a small camera. *These bitches are sitting back watching me.* Devilish thoughts cross my mind as I dance around the room like I'm at a strip club. I've never danced before, but have seen a lot of scenes on television, so I decide to give them a treat. "We Can Get It On" by Yo Gotti plays in my head as I swing my hips from left to right. I poke my ass out and take off my clothes one piece at a time. I start with my bra and panties, and my mind wonders if whoever is watching is hot and horny. I rub my naked pussy and play with my breasts. I bend over the small bed and make my ass cheeks slap together for a few minutes. Then I lay on the bed, and I dig two of my fingers into my pussy and play with myself. It starts out as a game, but it gets so good that I nut on myself. My body shakes and cum rolls off my fingers and onto the bed. Damn, that was a good nut.

After my short show, nobody bothers to come into the room and stop me. I put my clothes back on and am about to fall asleep when Nikki starts talking her all day, every day shit.

*****

“Dammit, you have got to get a grip. You’re acting like a weak muther-fucker,” I tell Nicole.

“I can’t help it. I’m so in love with Jeremy. Why did he hurt me?”

“He hurt you because he didn’t give a fuck, and that pussy-ass nigga is probably out now fucking the next bitch, while you’re up in here feeling sorry for yourself.”

“Help me, Nikki. I need you to be strong for me,” Nicole begs.

“I’m trying to be strong for you, but you keep fucking up. Stop all this muther-fucking crying like a baby. You’re a grown-ass woman. I’m so tired of the tears. If you keep crying, I will have to leave you,” I threaten.

“Please, Nikki! Don’t leave me! What will I do without you? I can’t survive without you,” Nicole shouts as she continues to cry.

“There you go again. All this fucking crying is unnecessary. I’m not going to leave you, but you must let me take control.”

“Okay Nikki. I will do whatever you say. Just don’t leave me alone.”

“I promise that we will always be together as one. We have been together all of our lives; there is no way I’m leaving. Just stop crying and be strong girl. Damn!”

“I love you so much Nikki. You know exactly what to say.”

“That’s why I am here…to love you and protect you. Right now, we have to figure out how in the hell we are going to break out of here.”

“Looks like we are stuck like Chuck,” Nicole jokes.

"Not for long, because I have a plan, so just focus on loving me, and I will find a way. Do you trust me?" I ask Nicole.

"I trust you Nikki," she replies.

I look around and realize that these walls are thick. I can't do a damn thing, so I scream and scream. My voice penetrates every room of the Raymond-Neal Psychiatric Hospital. I stop abruptly and begin to beat on the walls. Then, I run from wall to wall, ramming my body, trying to get out. Most of the walls don't affect me because they are padded, so I take it upon myself to start running into the steel door. *These bitches have to let me go,* I think as I scream and scream like someone is after me.

I have a few ideas of what to do in order to break out, but nothing concrete. *I can't believe these bitches locked me down. They think I'm fucking crazy, but they haven't seen anything yet.*

Chapter 1

As I screamed and banged on the muther-fucking walls, this small red-headed, freckle faced nurse rushed up to the door. She had a big-ass needle in her left hand, while two powerhouse nurses in white followed her like they were going to war or some shit. I was ready to get down because these bitches played dirty; they never came alone. I was taking a muther-fucker down if I didn't get out this bitch.

The sound of my voice continued to ring out. I looked up, and the nurse cracked open the door. Hurriedly, I shoved it towards her as if I was running for my life. She fell backwards and onto the floor. The two powerhouse nurses rushed up and shoved me back in as I swung like a wild, crazy bitch.

"Get off me bitch! I don't belong here! There has been a mistake!" I screamed.

"Hold her down! Hold her down! Hold her down!" the red-haired nurse yelled over and over, while rushing into the room like a mad scientist.

"I don't belong here! No! Stop! Quit! Let me go," I continued to yell as she shoved a big-ass needle into my right arm. Something started to happen. I suddenly felt like a sack of bricks. My voice became silent, and I stopped yelling. I glanced up and looked at the medicine being pushed into my arm. I felt like the walls were spinning, so I tried to fix my eyes on something, so I could stay alert, but the more I tried, the more the walls swayed back and forth. Unable to hold out, I smiled at Nicole as she turned around and walked deeper into the dark hole.

*****

Hours later, I came around. I moaned a little as I reached for my head. It ached so badly. I tried to open my eyes, but the walls were still spinning, so I closed them again.

"Let me try this again," I said as I opened my eyes once more. As I tried to focus, I looked over at the pure solid white walls. They looked like bubbles, the kind that keep sound in and everything else out. The new area caused me to sit up. I realized I was not in the same room. Those bitches had moved me yet again. To my far right, I saw the door; it looked like pure glass. Slowly, I turned my head. To my surprise, the whole front wall was made of glass.

When my head made it to the left, I noticed a black lady sitting there in a blue chair, watching me. She stared at me, and I stared back at her. I decided to get up. My balance was a little off, but I managed to stand. As my legs rocked a little, I looked back at the woman in the chair. She did not move, so I walked towards the door, and she did not try to stop me.

Before I could make it all the way to the door, the small red-headed lady appeared with a short, black female security guard. I looked at her as she motioned for me to stand back against the wall. I gave her a gaze that said I was ready to attack; however, the stare fazed her not. I turned around and stood against the wall.

"Are you better this morning?" she asked.

"Yes," I said. Then, I went straight to the point. "Why in the hell am I here?"

She was quiet. When she looked at me, I thought she rolled her eyes as she spoke, "You don't remember anything? We go through this every single day."

I glared at the nurse when she said "every single day".

"Every single day? How do we go through something every day, when I just got here?" I asked, while moving off the wall in a defensive motion.

"Get back on the wall," she demanded of me, but I became stubborn.

"Not until you tell me why I am here. I'm not fucking crazy, old lady. I have the right to know," I demanded of the nurse as the clicking noises invaded my head.

She dropped her head down. Then, she looked back at me and replied, "Why do you do this every day?"

"What do you mean? I thought I told you I just got here!" I yelled.

"You've been here almost a year, and, every day, your mind is blank. You don't remember anything we talk about." She came closer to me and whispered in my ear, "Don't play games with me, you schizophrenic bitch. Keep fucking with me, and I will get very angry."

I looked at her as she spoke those fighting words to me. I was not in a position to do anything, but, when I did get in a

position to do something, she'd better pray because it was either gonna be her ass or my freedom. I walked away from her. Then, it registered in my mind that she'd said a year, and all hell broke loose.

"Almost a year? Stop fucking lying! I just got here!" I screamed at her.

"Calm down! I'm not playing this game with you, Nicole. Since you still can't remember, open your mouth wide, so you can take this medicine," the nurse instructed.

"Bitch, I'm not taking a muther-fucking thing until you explain to me why the fuck I am here. I'm locked up like a caged animal, and you want to keep me doped up," I said.

As if she'd had enough of my mouth, she replied calmly, "You're in here for killing all those people."

Her accusation made my head snap upward. I replied with a confused look, "What people? You know what? I want to talk to my mother."

Very softly, she said, "Your mother is dead. You killed her."

I ran toward her, but the security guard stepped between us.

I said, "What? Bitch, you are fucking crazy. I didn't kill my mother."

"You killed your mother, your sister, and a lot of other people. Now, if you want to play crazy, play on your own time. Right now, you will sit your ass down and take this medicine."

"Bitch, I didn't kill anyone. My mother isn't dead. She is in New Castle, Washington. Somebody help me! This bitch is crazy!" I yelled as I tried to exit the door.

The security guard stepped in front of the door as I continued to yell louder and louder. While I faced the security guard, the nurse grabbed my arm. Anger overcame me, and I went fucking ballistic in that small confined room. I turned on her and rushed her so quickly that we both fell to the ground. The security guard tried to throw me with power as she tried to get me off the nurse.

I yelled and screamed, “I didn’t kill anyone!”

Somehow, my world felt like it had caved in on me, and the thought of killing people hurt me to my heart.

The nurse was pinned down under me, and the security guard kept trying to separate us. Then, I remembered that the nurse had been talking all that slick shit a few minutes ago, and, in that moment, she was about to feel the wrath of a woman that hated threats. I brought my mouth closer to her body and bit a huge plug out of her fucking neck. Blood gushed up in my face. Suddenly, a black stick was under my neck, choking the fuck out of me. I had to let go of the nurse as other security people with gloves on came in, yelling and running out of control. Blood oozed from my mouth as I became very violent and hysterical.

I felt this burning sensation hit my upper body; I looked down and saw this big-ass needle sticking out of my arm. I tried to grab the needle, but I could not. The white coats had me restrained, and one had hit me in the head. My head spun in fast circles, but I was aware of people rushing over to the nurse. I became disorientated, and, in that moment, my body fell to the floor. I saw the lights grow dimmer as I closed my eyes to sleep.

"Don't wake up. Don't wake up," was the voice I heard as I slowly moved my head to the left and partially opened my eyes. Through my limited vision, I saw a wall made of bubbles. It looked like the type you see when you open a wrapped package. I turned my head straight forward, and I saw a tinted glass wall. In the reflection, I saw myself in a white bed with a bandage wrapped on my head. I frowned from the pain, as I blinked my eyes twice.

I focused on the ceiling to try to get my eyesight together. Visions of Jeremy's cute face made me smile. His dimples, his laugh, and his beautiful eyes were so amazing to me. A love like his was to die for, and I was willing to do so. Memories came to mind of when we had laid on the couch and he had held me like a baby. We'd cradled each other, and it had made me feel like a million bucks. There was no love in this world better than his. He would learn to love me one day just as much as I loved him. Tears rolled down my face. I tried to wipe away the tears, but I realized I couldn't as I heard the sound of chains rattling. I snapped back to reality; I tried to focus on where the hell I was. I opened my eyes wider and tried to move my hands again, but something cool was pressing against my skin. I looked down and saw handcuffs.

I still did not know where I was. I turned my head to the right, saw a chair and remembered the nurse on the floor. I felt confused and subdued as I tried to move my legs but could not. At that moment, I became more confused and began to jerk and jerk, trying to free my hands.

Now, I was very alert and more confused than ever. I became frantic, and the moment I tried to speak out, a new nurse came in. She smiled and said, "I see you are awake, Ms. Nicole. Do you know where you are, now?"

Still not able to speak, I observed the nurse until I finally found my voice and asked, "Where am I?"

The nurse said, "You are in an asylum in Nevada."

Frowning at the word *asylum*, I looked puzzled and asked, "Why am I here? Why am I tied down? Can someone give me some answers?" I asked.

The nurse knew that she could not go further into detail, so she said, "Just relax, and the doctor will be in here in a few hours. Here is something to help you sleep."

Before I could tell the nurse that I didn't want any medicine, but wanted answers, she pulled out a big needle and jammed it into my arm. My eyes rolled into the back of my head; the lights went dim, and I thought, *I'm tired of all this damn sleeping*. I closed my eyes as my body relaxed.

A few hours later, when the doctor came in, I was wide awake. He was a white, blonde haired man with a small mustache and beard. He was very handsome and had a very bright smile. It wasn't a regular smile, but a smile that aroused the scent my body was giving off.

He came closer and said, "Hello, Nicole. I am Dr. John Adams, and I will be monitoring your progression to recovery."

He noticed that I was calm and that Nikki had not had time to resurface. Therefore, Dr. Adams summoned two gentlemen in all white clothing to unchain me, and they did. As they released me, I touched my wrists, then my head.

He said, "You will have a nasty bruise. Do you remember what happened, and why you are here?"

I looked at him with confusion and replied, "No, I don't quite know what happened. Will you tell me?"

He looked at me with concern and said, "Yes, I will tell you. You're in here because you are very ill. We need to help you get better."

"That doesn't explain how I got in here in the first place. You seem to think I need help for a reason. Why is that?" I asked.

He looked at me with a frown on his face as he replied, "I will explain, but I will have to handcuff you back down to the bed."

"Fuck no! I'm not getting tied back down. Why do I have to be tied down like a dog?"

"Because, every time we explain this to you, you go ballistic and get out of control. I can't have my patients upset and out of control. You will never recover that way. Just take your time and, when the time is right, I will let you know everything," he explained.

He looked at my chart and walked out. I just watched as he walked out the glass door. He hadn't explained a muther-fucking thing to me about why I was in there. I had a good idea, but I wanted him to tell me. As I paced the floor, I began to have flash backs. I stood in the middle of the floor, stared at the back of the room, and, in my mind's eye, I saw myself killing my mother. Then, the memory flashed to me, shooting my sister in the head. I'd killed so many people. I shook my head from left to right as I thought, *What in the hell have I done?* I'd lost my fucking mind all because of a broken heart. It was sad that love could make me kill. I put my head in my hands and cried. I sat down on the bed and put my head against the wall. More tears rolled down my face. I looked up, and I saw people walking my way. I immediately wiped my face, and the tears and self-pity vanished.

Within minutes, I was escorted to a room similar to the one I had just been in. The room was small with three gray, bubbly walls and one huge glass wall, so people could walk by and see you. I went to the bed. It looked uncomfortable, but I sat on it anyway and noticed that it was locked to the wall and had very thin white sheets on it. I laid back on the hard bed, and I saw one vent. *How funny?* I thought as I sat up on the bed. The door opened, and another caretaker walked in and said, "Group therapy starts in five minutes. Get ready to go in a few."

She closed the door and left.

Group therapy? I thought, *Why do I need to talk in a group? I am fine*.

Just like I was told, a nurse came in and took me to group therapy. I walked in and found that other women were there. Some looked spaced out. I felt uncomfortable around those loony toons. In fact, I felt scared out of my muther-fucking mind. Where in the fuck was Nikki? I was all alone in this whack ass place and I needed her to protect me from these crazy people.

Many of the bitches were talking to themselves; others were edgy and shit, as if they were on that fucking powder. I knew I was in the wrong place because of that damn Nikki.

The therapist spoke, "Acceptance is the first step to recovery. You must first admit there is a problem."

I looked around and said, "Ma'am, I don't have a problem. I am in the wrong place, and don't know why I am here. All you bitches are the ones who need help. Not me."

Those around me laughed, and I just stared because their laughs were really about to set me the fuck off.

The therapist asked, "Who is Nikki?"

I felt a tingle in my stomach and began to sweat when I heard her name. I looked stupidly at the therapist and lied, "I don't know who the hell she is. Is she the one I can talk to about getting out this muther-fucker? You WILL let me out, or I will shut it down up in here."

"Calm down Nicole," she stated.

"Is Nikki the reason I am here? If so, I need to talk to that bitch ASAP."

The therapist said, "Everyone here has a problem, and they must admit there is a problem. Talk to me when you remember who she is and why you are here. There is no time for games."

"Games? Bitch, I want out of here. I hate to get violent, but I will. Let me out," I threatened.

I looked at that bitch as if I wanted to jump, but I couldn't do it. Those bitches would lock me down for sure and drug the fuck out of me. I needed a clear head to figure out how I was going to break out of that bitch.

As I looked at the other participants, it appeared that they liked it there, but I had a lover waiting on me in my dreams, and I needed to talk to him. My mind had wandered about making love to Jeremy, when all of a sudden, I heard this stupid-ass female voice talking noise. My mind focused on what she was saying. A frown came over my face, and I looked at her sideways.

This brown haired older lady said authoritatively, "Why are you acting so stupid? You know you stalked this Jeremy dude, and he didn't want your crazy ass."

"Shut the fuck up! You clearly don't know what the hell you're talking about," I responded.

"You killed all these people over a nigga that didn't want your weak ass. Then, you had the nerve to kill your own mama. I salute you," she said as she raised her hand to her forehead.

"Take it back," I replied as I got up out of my seat and walked over to her.

"Sit down Nicole. Ladies, calm down and take a breather," the therapist spoke from across the room.

I returned to my seat, and the lady continued as she sat there, "Truth hurts. A piece of shit like you belongs in here. You're a crazy. Shit, they say we're all crazy. Sit your crazy ass down."

I heard clicking noises in my head. The noise banged louder and louder as my blood came to a boil. My body had grown very hot, so I stood up again. *Click, click, click*. So many things were rushing through my head. I wanted to dig her fucking eyeballs out, or pull her hair out at the roots, or possibly bite her muther-fucking nose off. I could actually see myself taking my fists and beating her head into the concrete until she couldn't move. Fuck it! I was tired of listening to this muther-fucker. Before that bitch said another word, I showed her.

"You better leave me the fuck alone, or I will hurt you," I said.

"I am not afraid of you. What're you going to do? Kill me too?" she replied.

"I'm not going to kill you, but you're going to wish you were dead," I shot back.

"Ladies, calm down! Nicole, sit down!" the therapist interrupted.

"Fuck you!" I spoke to the older lady.

Without warning and with my left foot flat on the floor, I lifted my right leg and kicked that big mouth bitch evenly in her muther-fucking chest. The force of my foot rocked her head so hard that she fell backwards. I thought I'd broken that bitch's neck. Her body went down in slow motion. Once her body had hit the floor, everyone got up and ran towards the door. I just stood there, looking at the older lady as she lay on the ground. Two security guards rushed in as the therapist grabbed me by my shirt and pulled me backwards. I didn't put up a fight; I just did as she directed me.

The older lady jumped up from the floor, yelling and screaming at me, as if she was ready to throw down. The security guards grabbed her as the therapist held me against the wall. I didn't move. In fact, I couldn't move. I was numb, so I just stood there like a zombie, unemotional and unfeeling. The security guards carried the old mental patient out of the room. The group therapist turned around and looked at me. Then, she said, "Can you stop being violent for one day? Don't you know that the more you act out, the longer you stay here?"

I looked at her with a straight face and replied, "No, I can't. I have so much anger and hate in me that quitting seems to be the last thing I will do."

"I understand that, but you can't stay angry forever. You have to forgive and forget," she explained.

"I will forgive when all those that hurt me are dead. I will not stop this until the day I die. And I'm ready to die," I spoke as I looked her straight in the face.

The look she had on her face was void and confused. She turned away from me and shook her head. During this time, the small, black, female security guard and two male nurses escorted me back to my room. *Click, click, click.*

*****

"Nikki, you have messed up things in here for me. Now, this crazy-ass therapist really thinks I'm crazy. It's not me, it's you," I said.

"Nicole, as far as I'm concerned, we both are crazy in case you didn't notice. It is time for me to come out and show you just how to live. The image you are giving us is pathetic and pitiful. You saw how I had to step in and put those self-righteous bastards in their place," I replied with no fear.

"I will not let you take over our life and destroy it. I just can't," Nicole said.

"How in the fuck are you going to stop me? Just remember, I'm running this show, not you. You brought me into your life. I didn't bring you into mine."

"Nikki, I'm so tired of you throwing that up in my face," Nicole whined.

"So, who gives a fuck about what you're tired of?" I remarked while turning away from her.

Before I could do anything else, my body started shaking, and spit formed in the corner of my mouth. I fell to the floor, and my hands rammed themselves against my body and face violently. Every time I tried to move, my own limbs would abuse me more. I attempted to crawl to the door, but my legs felt like dead weight. Somehow, my body turned over, and my stomach tightened.

"What is going on?" I yelled out, but no nurse or caretaker came to my aid.

Suddenly, my eyes felt heavy, and my arms went weightless. I heard the taunting words I only heard in my head sometimes. "Nobody's going to help you, Nicole. Bitch, you're going to die. I won't stop until I squeeze the life from your body. I'm taking over. You can't handle the pressure anymore. Just leave it all to me."

All I could do was cry. The dark side was taking over, and there was nothing I could do.

Chapter 2

I woke up this morning with a new lease on life. That weak bitch Nicole was now in *my* head. I had to come forth and shown her how she really needed to do things. I'd let her run our life for too long. She had become frail and easy to the game. I intended to get us back on top and down for whatever, at any cost.

It was time for lunch. I was not hungry, but I needed to start getting things in motion. Nicole might have wanted to stay in here, but not me. I had to put my feet on the ground and make shit happen.

As I checked out all the crazies in this damn place, I set my sights on a window seat. The view allowed me access to observe how the daily operations went. I placed my lunch tray down on the table and pulled out a seat. A lady dressed in a white coat came over and nicely said, "Hello Nicole."

I did not respond to her. I turned my head away from her and looked out the window at the new nurses coming into the building.

"Today is my first day here on the job, and I will be your new doctor. May I sit with you for a moment or two?" she pressed.

Without waiting on me to respond, she sat down with a lunch tray and proceeded to eat as if we were old friends or something. I looked at that stupid muther-fucker as if she was crazy. I didn't want her to be my doctor; I wanted Dr. Adams, not her. *I wonder where the fuck he is at. Why did they trade him for another doctor?* I thought as I eyed her up and down.

She continued, "Why are you here? Let me rephrase that. Why do you think you are here, Nicole?"

I said, "I don't know, but can someone give me an answer? Why won't you tell me about my prognosis, doctor?" I replied.

The doctor leaned closer and said, "A family trauma or the hurt from a loved one. In your case, the hurt from many loved ones. All that pain, neglect, and abuse made you do things and hear things you ordinarily would not have. From your charts and from what I know of your situation, I would say you have a split personality, and to me, that is a sign of schizophrenia or bipolar disorder. Pick one."

In a deeper tone, I said, "You don't know a damn thing about what I have been through in my life. You have no idea about the things that have wounded me or know about the loves in my life. Lady, I don't hear voices, and nothing is telling me or has told me to do anything, but you better step the fuck off. Better yet, get your ass up from my table."

She ate a few more bites of her sandwich and sipped some of her milk. The female doctor then penetrated me with a deep stare. After placing both of her elbows on the table, she said, "Nicole, Nikki, or whoever you are today and whatever you were last week, I recognize my own kind."

I could not even respond because I did not understand what she meant by "I recognize my own kind." At that moment, two men dressed in white, whom I had seen earlier, approached the table. I looked up at them as the smallest of the two said, "Diane, didn't we warn you about stealing the doctors' coats and pretending to be them?"

My mouth fell open. I'd thought this slow bitch was a real doctor. She'd fooled the fuck out of me. The bitch was a damn good actress. I had to give her that. With a covert frown, I glanced up at her and replayed the whole conversation in my mind. As I replayed it, a heavy rage invaded my head. One of the men took the coat as this girl Diane looked at me. She raised her brow, jumped up, and ran away. Furious about being gamed, I stood up from the table and was ready to go H.A.M., but one man shoved me back down into my seat, while the other man went after her. I wanted to beat the fuck out of that bitch for tricking me. I would see that whore on the flip side. This time, I would let her ride; fake-ass, muther-fuckin' loony tune.

That night, I laid on my back and stared at the white ceiling. I could not sleep at first because I was still baffled by how the girl Diane had pretended to be a medical professional. If it had not been for the nurses coming over, I would have believed her one hundred percent. I closed my eyes, turned onto my side, and tried to go to sleep, but that did not help. I turned on my other side and closed my eyes again. This time, when sleep did visit me, I dreamed an exciting dream.

Jeremy was kissing me feverishly as we were leading up to making love. His touch was a little off, but I did not allow that to stop me from wanting him more. "I hope he gets me pregnant this time," I thought, but he seemed to not have his mind on making love, so I asked him between my deep breaths, "Baby, are you okay? You seem preoccupied with something."

"Nicole, I need to tell you something," he said as he looked into my eyes.

"Can't it wait? I do need to feel you deep within me," I said as I kissed him to get his mind off of whatever it was he wanted to tell me.

He pulled away and said, "Yes, it can wait. I need to feel myself deep inside you, too."

We resumed kissing, but it seemed like his first time because he looked nervous. Jeremy got on top of me, and his body molded to my body perfectly. He took my breath away when he entered me forcefully. The shock wore off as my pussy juice increased for him. The love of my life, my best friend, made me feel loved for many hours. He was making this time more special than any time we had ever made love. It was as if I had never experienced so much love coming from him. He took his time to please me in every single way possible. Jeremy did not stop until I was flooded with complete satisfaction and overflowed with the love he had inside for me. Each thrust and movement was anticipated and enjoyed as he completed me to the max. Once we finished making love, I laid in his arms, but his mind seemed to be somewhere else. He looked at me as he said, "Nicole, you are an amazing woman, and it is not because we made passionate love."

I felt like something was wrong, so I sat up and stared at him.

"Tonight was our last time making love," he continued.

"What do you mean 'our last time making love'?" I asked as many thoughts poured into my mind.

"We will have to go back to being friends and nothing more," he said as he got out of bed and began to put on his clothes.

"Wait one damn minute! You mean to tell me that tonight meant nothing to you, and after what we just shared, you've decided we only need to be friends?" I asked as my nerves tingled.

"Nicole, I tried to tell you, but you insisted I wait," he replied.

"Fuck yeah! You already had me turned on and overheating for you. Why didn't you tell me this before we started making love?" I said as I felt the tears swelling in my eyes.

"I guess a part of me wanted to make our last time more meaningful," he said as he put on his shirt and looked down at me still on my elbows in the bed.

"In other words, you used me," I said harshly.

"Come on, Nicole. Tonight, we used each other. You needed me as much as I needed you, so you are just as much to blame as I am."

"No Jeremy. You knew beforehand, but I didn't think you had anything important to say, like always. So, I brushed it off as one of those times. Tonight Jeremy, you showed your ass in bed, and after taking me for that ride, you are still showing your ass by taking my emotions for another ride. Please don't do this to me, to us. I love you," I begged.

Jeremy glared at me as he smashed my heart, "Nicole, let us just enjoy what we had and let that be it. I will only be your friend and nothing more."

He walked out the door and out of my life. I could have died right then and there because the man I loved did not love me back. I sat back on my bed and let the tears stream down my face, for nothing could have prevented the pain I was feeling. I thought about everything he and I had done together. The tears continued as I turned over and cried harder. With my hand, I touched the spot where he had just laid, and I could still smell his presence. My heart shattered more because I knew Jeremy, and if he said friends, then that is what he meant. He would not go back on his word because he was that type of guy. Now, that type of guy had hurt me beyond imagination, and my life seemed unfixable to me. The more the tears came, the more my stomach tied in knots.

After many, many hours and days of being depressed and hurt, the feelings of love began to leave. I tried to hold on as long as I could, but after a while, I could not. Unleashing and letting him feel the pain was now my plan for Jeremy. I now looked at him with nothing but full blown rage. The feeling of love I once had was now gone, and payback was the only thing on my mind. I imagined myself slicing and dicing at him with a huge knife. In my fantasy, after I finished cutting his body up to nothing, I cried at his feet. That lying son-of-a-bitch had hurt me, and he had to die for causing me grief and pain.

Suddenly, I opened my eyes. My lips were trembling, and tears were on my cheeks. My body temperature had spiked, and sweat covered my hands and brows. I knew right then, every damn single thing that had happened to me before I got to the asylum. My pulse raced, and my mind ran like a fire on wheat and dry grass. My breath quickened as I closed my sweaty fists and thought of the betrayal. My anger was now real and roaring like a hungry lion. I finally said, "You will regret the day you walked on my feelings and tore out my heart."

I got up, and my thoughts turned to that punk-ass Cowboy. I touched the back of my head where he had hit me. *How the fuck did I not see that bastard coming up behind me?* I pondered that as I continued pacing the floor harder. I went deeper into thought. I stood by the bed and remembered the facial expressions I'd seen on Jeremy's face as I was about to kill him. I sat down again and remembered how stunned he had been to see me there, ready to end his life like he'd ended mine.

I stood up and paced the floor again. The more I thought about it, the more I became aroused with passion to settle the score with Jeremy, the one who'd broken Nicole's heart again. I had already evened the score with my first true love, Marvin. He was dead, and now, Jeremy had to die. I would not stop until that nigga's body was laying in front of me. I placed my hands under my head as I laid back down on the bed. I crossed my feet and decided that, before I killed Jeremy, I would make him suffer for hurting me. *Nobody hurts me and gets away with it. Nobody.*

Over the next few days, I played it nice and continued to be a good girl. Whenever Nicole tried to resurface, I would think about Jeremy and everyone else because the pain they had given me got me very angry. And, when I am outraged, Nicole cannot come near me, for I am the product of her hate. I had to make sure that that fucking Nicole laid her ass down. I pretended for the doctors that I was changing and that all their treatments were really working.

Every day at lunch, I would seek out the lady that had pretended to be a doctor. I listened to her snitch like a little bitch on the other patients. She'd tell who was doing what and where in the facility. She knew some of the doctors she met often fucked the patients. The patients couldn't snitch because no one would believe them, or the doctor would have them in lockdown before the truth made it to the top. To me, that was all I needed to know, and besides that, I found that playing the system would work to my advantage.

It was late at night and *Click, click, click* was now ringing in my head. I tried to retain her to just a mere thought, but, that night, she was strong, and I had to let her speak.

"You are going to be finished. Wait until I regain my strength and pride," Nicole said to me.

"Nicole, you do know that I can hear you talk and think shit about me? You want to do this and that, but the truth be told, you only bump your gums and get on my damn nerves," I replied to her.

"One of these days, I will do more than just talk. Best believe that," Nicole said to me.

"Bitch, you are the weakest link... Goodbye! You should have kept your damn heart in your damn chest, but no, you wanted to give it away. And now, look. We are in this muther-fucking crazy house because of you and that pitiful-ass Jeremy.

Speaking of Jeremy, when I get out, I'm gonna kill him," I said and did not care if she liked it or not.

"No, Nikki! I can't let you kill Jeremy. Hurting him is one thing, but to kill him is another thing." Nicole said to me forcefully.

"Shut the fuck up. You do realize that we are in a fucking nuthouse. Do you or do you not see these crazy mutherfuckers up in here? I know you don't think your ass has good sense and everybody else is fucked up. Think again. We are here, but unlike them, we will get the fuck out. So don't worry. Let me get this plan in gear."

"Nikki, I don't want to leave right now," Nicole replied, sounding scared.

"You stupid bitch!" I yelled at her and then said harshly, "I'm not going to let you or anyone ruin my plans to escape."

"I can't let you do this Nikki. Jeremy is the love of my life, and I refuse to let you hurt him," Nicole said.

"I'm running this show. I've heard enough about you and this fucking Jeremy. Remember, you loved Marvin too, and that bitch is dead."

Those clicking noises started sounding off over and over again in my head. *Click, click, Click.* I began to get very angry at Nicole. I screamed at her, and that underhanded bitch hit me in my damn mouth with her right hand. I grabbed her by the hand and twisted it. She cried out in pain, but I was angry. I caught her off-guard and tripped her. She looked shocked that I would flip her, but she was trying to put me back in her mind, and no way was I going to let that happen.

Before she knew what was going on, I took my hands and began making a believer out of that weak bitch. With every ounce of anger in me, I bounced that bitch's head on the floor until I saw blood rush from the side of her head. She jumped up on me but did not stay up there long. I rammed that muther-fucking head of hers straight into that thick glass door. *BAM* was the loud sound her damn head made. I watched Nicole as she lay on the floor, with her head bleeding like a gutted hog.

The nurses must have heard the commotion. They came to her rescue before I could do more bodily harm to her. *I bet she now knows that she can't play with everyone and get away with it, especially her own self*, I thought. I didn't give a fuck. This bitch was getting in my way, and I had to stop her ASAP.

Chapter 3

The two powerhouse nurses rushed me to the residential hospital. My head was spinning like a muther-fucker, and I could not make out what all was going on with me. As they rushed me to the hospital ward, I laid on the hospital bed, looking at bright lights and listening to the sounds of different people.

I did not care where they were taking me. All I knew was that I needed some help, and medicine was not the cure. My body ached, and my head throbbed from the fight I'd had with Nicole. My thoughts were only of this Nicole. As much as I had been hurt, while lying on the hospital bed, I could still feel the tension between us growing ever so strong, but I would do whatever it took to stop this pussy-ass bitch from coming back. I was sure she now saw that I controlled our lives, and when I was in control, things ran smoothly. Therefore, I had no doubt that it was time for me to get outside and track Jeremy down and kill anyone that got in my fucking way. If it came down to it, I would kill Nicole too. Thinking of evil and rage caused my body to feel better. My head no longer ached, and the ass whipping that had gone on in the room became irrelevant. Pain was gone, and getting even was the thing that drove my body to feel better.

I heard one of the two men tell me to raise my body and to scoot on the count of three, and I did. After they put me on the bed, I just laid there at first. Then, it hit me that the hospital ward was next door to the entrance that the employees used to go and come. Nicole did not want me to get up, but after lying on the bed for many minutes, I found the strength. I got up and peeped from behind the curtains. Things were out of order, and everything around me appeared bleak. People were everywhere, and I noticed that the shift was changing. A devilish smile lifted my face because the shift change was why everything was the way it was. I saw a nurse coming my way, so I ran back to the bed and laid down. Moments later, the nurse came in. She looked at my chart and put it back down. She came closer to me and only looked at me before leaving the room.

Then, she came back in. Now, it was time for me to act my ass off. I lifted my head up, placed my right hand on my forehead and partially closed my eyes. She came over to me and placed her hand on my back. I forced myself to get on up, swung my legs over the side of the bed and looked around before saying, "Nurse, I need to go to the bathroom."

She looked around nervously as I continued to stare at her. I sized her up to be a new hire because an old hand would know not to be left alone with one of us unguarded, and it was the middle of a shift change. This was my window of opportunity because this nurse was perfect. She was a young nurse and about my height and hair color. The only difference was I had a bandage on my head. I could tell that she did not know what to do.

"You need to go to the bathroom?" she asked, looking around helplessly.

I glanced at her name tag and saw it read LISA. I continued to play hurt and injured. I looked back at the woman's face and replied anxiously, "Yes, ma'am. Please help me. I can't hold it much longer."

The nurse's eyes roamed the room again, and I knew she was debating if she should do it or not, so, I spoke sadly, "No one will know you helped me go to the bathroom. What damage could I do in the bathroom?"

Without replying, she came closer and responded, "Okay. Make it quick."

After we walked to the bathroom, Nurse Lisa waited for me outside while I went into the stall. I observed that I was there alone. I carefully took off my bandage, sat naked on the toilet and patiently waited for her to check on me, and like clockwork, she did.

"You alright in there?" she asked as I saw her feet walking towards my stall.

I did not answer because I needed her to come closer to me and become entangled in the web I was spinning. When she came closer, my quick reflexes allowed me to slam the door in her face. When the nurse fell, I straddled her and banged her fucking head on the floor until she was out cold. I quickly undressed her, took off her uniform, and put it on. I bent back down and put my gown on her as she laid there helplessly. I pulled the nurse's hat farther down on my head, walked out of the bathroom, and straight past the other newly hired nurses as they scanned their ID badges.

Stepping outside the Raymond Neil Psychiatric Ward was wonderful to me. The sun had never shone so brightly. The wind had never blown so gently, and the air was so clean and pure. Once I was outside the walls for the first time in almost a year, it pleased me so much to finally be free. I focused my thoughts because I was not totally free yet. I noticed the employees were all going to their vehicles, so, unsuspected, I approached a white nurse.

"Excuse me," I said in a polite voice. When she turned around, I saw her nametag read CONNIE.

"Hey there, Co-worker Lisa. How's it going with you today?" she asked as she smiled sweetly.

"My ride is late, and I was wondering if I could ride with you as far as you are going?" I replied.

"You sure can. Let me unlock the door and we can get going," she said with joy in her voice.

The feelings of nervousness kept me looking around. I kept thinking that someone had noticed the switch up. However, no one came. When I opened the door and sat in her car, relaxation and pleasure overwhelmed me. I was so excited. Her irritatingly cheery voice broke into my thoughts.

She asked, "Where you from?"

"I graduated from North Carolina State University, so I claim North Carolina as my home," I said, lying with a straight face.

"Well, I am from Montana. Cat's Cave, Montana to be exact, where everybody loves everybody."

"Must be nice to be from a place like that," I commented, hoping the conversation would cease, but the talking and conversation kept on coming at me.

"You like working around all those people? Because I do," Connie said.

"It is okay, just a job," I said in a low tone.

"It's okay? It is more than okay," she said excitedly.

"These people need our help to function in society. It is wonderful to help those that need our help. Don't you think so?" she paused to glance at my name tag again. Then, she said, "Lisa?"

"Yeah, those crazies do need our help, don't they?" I said, planning the perfect spot to have her pull over.

"Will you be alright if I stop in the store for a second?" she asked as she slowed down and turned in anyway.

When the naïve nurse got out, I searched her glove compartment. A smile crossed my face when my hands rubbed the blade of a butcher's knife. In haste, I put the knife in my right hand and held it in my hand by the door.

When she got back in the car, we drove off. It'd been a year, but I kind of knew the area well. I knew a back road was up ahead, so I said to her, "You can turn down the very next driveway. Thank you for allowing me to ride in your car. I really appreciate it."

"Anytime! If I can help, I will," she said as she drove a mile before the turn came up.

"Slow down. I stay down this road," I said, and she turned down the wagon road.

"You sure you stay back here? It is kind of dark and scary," she said with uncertainty.

"Yeah. Just stop here, and I can walk the rest of the way," I said, easing my knife up in attack mode.

She turned on the interior light and responded, "You sure? I don't mind taking you further down the driveway."

With unbridled force and anger, I replied, "Didn't I say stop here?"

Before she could respond, I pounced on her and plunged the knife into her chest several times. I got out the car, went to the driver's side of the car, and opened the door.

She turned her head towards me. As her eyes bucked and her body trembled, she tried to speak. I looked at her and said, "I'm sure you want to know why I have done this to you, and, since you are about to die, I guess I can tell you. I killed you for your ride, bitch! Get the fuck out!"

After I told her that, I pulled her out the car and dragged her light body by the hair into the secluded woods. She did not put up a fight because her body was lifeless, and to me, meaningless. I saw a big hole in the ground, and I threw her body in it. Then, I dusted my hands off and walked back to the car.

I opened the trunk and discovered an overnight bag filled with clothes. I unzipped the bag and used some sanitizer I had also discovered to remove the blood from my hands and face. I pulled my hair into a ponytail, dug around in the bag more, took out the clothes I had found and put them on. After getting dressed, I tossed my bloody clothes into the woods on top of her. They weren't going to benefit me by dragging them around.

I looked towards the spot I had thrown the nurse and said, "Bitch, I'm so glad you have clothes that fit me. How lucky is that?"

I fastened the pants and shirt. I picked up a towel, closed the trunk, poured the sanitizer on the towel and cleaned up the driver's side of car. When I finished, I closed the door and threw the bloody towel on the ground by the back tire. Then, I sat back in the driver's seat and closed my eyes. I rested there for a few minutes. I almost had a fucking heart attack, moments later, when I was disturbed by a knock on the window. When I opened my eyes, it was Connie. I jumped back because seeing her scared the fuck out of me. I'd thought she was dead. Before I could react, she reached back and busted the driver's window. While grabbing the knife, I quickly moved to the passenger side of the car and jumped out that muther-fucker.

"Damn bitch! You came back from the dead?" I spoke nervously but laughed at the same time.

She appeared extremely weak, but she had enough strength to hold a tire iron upright like she was going to hit me.

"I gave you a ride, and you tried to kill me! How could you?" she said with blood and dirt gathered on her chest area.

I ducked down by her car and picked up some soil. I lifted my head back up and replied, "I told you I wanted your fucking car. This time, I will not fail."

I got close enough and then threw dirt in her face.

The dirt distracted her, so I jumped on her like a cheetah pouncing on a zebra. She dropped the tire iron and fell back on the ground. I dropped the knife and grabbed the tire iron and started hitting her in her face over and over as she tried to fight back again. Then I dropped the tire iron, picked up the knife again, and stabbed her in the face a couple of times. I stabbed her in the top of her head and sliced down, splitting her face in half. I continued sitting on her and kept stabbing her face and chest. I had to make sure she did not come back from the grave again.

"Bitch, now I have to find some more of your clothes to put on," I said as I got off her and waited until my breathing returned to normal.

I pulled her body to the front of her car and then walked to the back of the car. I got out another one of her outfits, sanitized myself, and put it on. I tossed the bloody clothes on her dead body. Then, I got a little angry because fucking around with this bitch had caused me to lose two outfits that I might've needed to use later on.

I closed the trunk, cleaned off the steering wheel, and got in the car. I put the car in drive and drove over her body several times. I laughed at the new meaning she gave to "over my dead body". After the last time I drove over her, I continued on down the driveway but stopped a few feet from the paved road to rest for a few more minutes. However, I couldn't take too long because I had to get the fuck out of there. Those fucking people would be looking for me like buzzards circling over a dead cow. As I laid my head back on the head rest, I thought I heard my name on the radio. I turned the radio up and heard the announcer say, "Attention, all residents of Las Vegas. A patient has escaped from the Raymond Neil Psychiatric Institution. Her name is Nicole Webb, but she is also referred to as Nikki Webb, and she is very, very dangerous. We believe the patient is on foot. She is dressed as a nurse, wearing an all-white uniform. Nicole Webb is an African-American female. She has a caramel brown complexion and shoulder length hair. Warning: She is very dangerous. If anyone comes across this patient, do not attempt to subdue her. Call the police immediately. Again, call the police immediately."

I sat up straight and looked around. It wouldn't be long before the Nevada State Police, the Las Vegas Metropolitan Police, the Raymond Neil Police, and the Clark County Sheriff's Department would be after my ass. I had to hurry up and leave Las Vegas. I didn't need this kind of heat because I had to find Jeremy before these bitches tried to take me out. One thing I had learned was that the police would kill you. They wouldn't ask questions later and definitely wouldn't give a fuck. I needed to leave, but I also needed to rest. So, I laid back on the head rest again and tried to relax. As I dozed, I started to dream.

Chapter 4

I was a young girl, playing in my room. My sister was gone and I was alone, as usual. I got tired of playing alone, so I looked in the mirror. I stared at my sad reflection and said, "If I had my own best friend to play with, her name would be Nikki. She would not let anyone push me around, and she would make my life happier."

I closed my eyes and crossed my fingers, but she did not come alive like my sister had said she would. Vanessa lied, I thought.

Despite that, every day for the next five months, I sat there in front of the mirror waiting on my best friend to come. Then one day, she came. I was alone when I heard her speak to me for the first time.

*****

Click, click, click. The loud sound woke me up, and I heard the familiar sounds in my head as my hands rushed to encompass the pain that invaded it.

"I can't just let you show up when you want to Nicole. I run things now," I said to her.

I kept my eyes closed and tried to ignore the clicking in my head. I opened my eyes and placed my hands on each side of my head again. That did not work, so I removed my hands, shook my head and let my eyes shake as my brain rattled. These sounds were more intense than they used to be. For a moment, they stopped, but as soon as I thought they were gone, I heard the *click, click, click* sounds again. This time, I sat up in the driver's seat. I looked at the fronts and backs of my hands. I turned to the side of me and saw Nicole staring back at me. Without hesitation, I hollered at the sight because I thought I'd gotten rid of her. *When will this bitch leave me alone? Reality is I might have to take her out of the game. It's checkout time,* I thought to myself.

I started up the car and recalled that Jeremy had family in Utah. I drove off and headed down the street away from the crime scene, like the muther-fucking law wasn't looking for me, and I began my journey to Cedar City, Utah.

"Nikki calm down! You didn't have to kill her!"

I looked over at her and said, "You dumb bitch. I'm a survivor, unlike you."

"Nikki, I will not allow you to ruin my life," she responded.

"Ya ya ya ya ya!. Here you go again, saying that you won't allow me to ruin your life. Don't you ever get tired of repeating yourself? You ought to listen to yourself. Every time I do something you don't like, you complain and start running off at the damn mouth. Do you ever say any muther-fucking thing differently, or is 'I won't allow you to ruin my life' the only tune you know?"

"People like you have to be kept in check. You need to know that you are not in this alone. It is not just your life. Your actions affect me as well. I'm the one that gets in trouble when you decide to do something," Nicole replied.

"Your life? You muther-fucking bitch, you had no life until I showed up and showed your bitch ass how to live. All you did before me was sit in front of a mirror and pout. You had no spunk about yourself. You were a follower and not a leader, so shut the fuck up talking to me," I spat out angrily.

As I returned my eyes to the road, Nicole said, "How to live? You mean how to kill. That is all you have done Nikki. Anyone who has a different way of thinking from yours will be dead, right?"

"Pretty much. Because it is my way or the highway. Anything else can be left on the side of the damn road for garbage day," I said to Nicole as she listened without commenting.

As I drove further down the highway, I tried to ignore Nicole, but she kept running off at the mouth.

"Listen to me. Stop your deceit, lies, and hurting people, Nikki. Let's go back to how we used to be," Nicole implored.

"How in the fuck can we do the things we used to do? Do you realize that we have broken out of a fucking nut house? All of this is happening because of me. I do the things you only dream of doing," I retorted.

"Nikki, you are better than what you give people," Nicole said.

"If I was better, then you would be the one that ceases to exist, and not me," I said to her with disappointment.

"You can either get on board with the takeover that's coming for us to get help, or we will both die in vain, and I will make sure of that. If it's the last thing I do, I WILL stop you where you stand one day," Nicole said with conviction.

Looking over at Nicole, I replied with anger as I drove with my left hand on the wheel and my right hand banging on the dashboard, "Ha! You stop me? Bitch, you must be crazy! It will be a cold day in hell before you defeat me. Hear me? I'll kill you before I let you stop me."

"Nikki, what are we doing out here? You don't know how to just let things go. You take it to the extreme. You can't fix all of our problems, but some improvement beats no improvement. I wanted you to come in and help me, not take over and make my life miserable," Nicole said boldly, seemingly a different person that the righteous leader that just threatened to get rid of me.

As I drove faster, I screamed my damn head off as I replied to the cocky bitch, "Let it go? After all the bullshit we've been through, you want me to let that shit ride? I don't think so. Leave me the fuck alone and get off my ass. You need me. You need me to keep things operating well in your life. If you hadn't needed me, then I would not exist."

"Nikki, I am you, and you are me. You desire to control me, but you need to understand that our outlooks on things are totally opposite from anything in the world. You could not have an identity without me. I desire love, and you don't. You love to kill, and I don't. See the differences between us? I do. "

"We are totally different, but we are together as one," I said as I drove like a maniac. "I could never be anything like you. This world is not big enough for two weak, pathetic-ass fools."

"Are you trying to get rid of me?" Nicole asked solemnly.

"Trying to get rid of you? I *am* you, but you can never get on my level. I tell you what..."

I pulled to the side of the street slowly. I stared into the eyes of the weakling who was speaking without authority and said, "Shut the fuck up! I am running this damn show! You can either get right or get fucking left!"

I then banged on the dashboard, trying to scare Nicole. I turned up the music, stepped on the gas, and peeled out.

I drove around in a daze, as if nothing mattered anymore. My head was aching, so I yelled at the pain, "Get out of my head! You make me sick! I hate you! I really hate your guts bitch!" but the pain lingered with me.

As I looked for a place to rest, my mind went blank, and before I knew it, I was staring at Jeremy's old vacant house. I could see him and me sitting on the steps, chatting like old times and drinking lemonade. I parked on the street with the other cars and stared harder at the house. I got out the car with my knife hidden and walked up to the old house. I looked around to see if anyone was looking or if the police were on my tail. I walked up to the door, and after taking another look around to see if any nosey neighbors were out, I used my left hand to bust the small glass out of the door. As I reached in to unlock the door, I scraped my knuckles. I used my tongue to taste the sweet blood, and immediately licked and smacked my lips. I then looked up and before my eyes... *I can see Jeremy and me, sitting at the kitchen table, sharing dinner. He laughs at something I've said. "How in love we seem," I think as I reminisce. I allow my eyes to take me further, as he and I get up and walk into the living room. I follow closely behind the daydream, and I step into the living room. There, we cuddle as we watch a movie. He feeds me popcorn, and I feed him some back. Jeremy laughs as he pulls me closer and squeezes me tenderly. I close my eyes and wrap my arms around myself. I can actually feel his massive hands upon my body, touching me with love as his fingers glide down my body. Warm sensations cross me as I feel his arms embracing me. He and I get up and walk down the hall. I know exactly where we are going because we are alone. I, in haste, run down the hall to his bedroom. I hear my voice tell him to give me more. As I open the door, I see he is on top of me, making love to me, and before his orgasm, he tells me he loves me as he plunges deeper into me. I stand back as I watch the lovemaking he and I share. From this view, he is massive and very much in control of delivering to me the pleasure he had already given many times before. I walk closer to where the bed once was and lay on the floor. I smile as I turned my head over to see Jeremy next to me. I reach over to touch his face, and he disappears. The smile disappears from my face. I close my eyes tight and fall asleep in the hopes of dreaming more.*

*****

My dream was not at all like I wanted it to be. I dreamed about the time my mother tried to kill me. She was a selfish and mean ass hoe. How in the hell could my father have loved her? He must have been crazy too.

"Go get in the tub. It is bath time for you," my mother says.

I go into the bathroom and notice that the water was higher than before, but I strip anyway. As I remembered the feeling of the semi-cool water on my skin, I shuttered in my sleep. *I step deeper into the water and laugh because my favorite toy is upside down at the bottom of the tub. I reach for it and begin to play with it. I hear something at the door, so I look up to see it was Mother. She has a strange look on her face as her eyes land upon me in the water, but I ignore it and play with the toy.*

She comes closer to me and sits on the toilet at first. I glance up and into her face and see she is not smiling. Mother then turns the water on, and watches as it rises higher. I look into her face again, and she turns the water off. Mother gets up and sits behind me on the edge of the tub. She started splashing water on me in small scoops, but for some reason, this gives me an awkward feeling. When she starts talking to me, I stop playing and listen.

"You know Nicole, my life has changed, and it is because of you, all because of little Nicole."

"Mother, we have all changed since Daddy went away," I say in my sad, childlike voice.

"Yes, went away," she says as she nods her head in an odd way.

"But bad girls have to be punished. Don't you agree Nicole?" Mother continues from her seat on the tub's edge, before scooting closer to me.

I lift up my head and speak over my shoulder to her, "No Mother! Please don't. I will be a good girl. I promise. I didn't mean to stand there and not go get help for Daddy."

My mother stares at me and then vindictively asks, "You know it was your fault that your daddy died, don't you?"

I weep uncontrollably as I speak to her, "I said I was sorry. I know it was my fault Daddy died. He's in heaven now with God."

Mother gets in front of me and slaps my face as I cry. She leans closer to me and says, "There is no God where you are going, you dirty little bitch."

In an instant, she pushes me backwards, and water surrounds me. I kick and try to remove her hands from me, but she is too strong. I feel numb as my eyes close, but, from under the water, I hear Vanessa scream, "Let her go, Mom! You will go to jail, and I will be all alone!"

I open my eyes to see my mother look back at my sister. She, then looks at me before letting me go. My body jerks up and out of the water as I gasp for air. I cough uncontrollably. My breath comes back to me slowly as I stare at the two. I am hurt because my mother stopped because my sister does not want to be alone. A look of pain is on my face as I watch them acting so happy.

I stare at them both as Mother says with hate, "One day, you will pay for making me live alone."

*****

My eyes popped open. I twisted my head from left to right. I snapped back to reality and realized where I was. I was still at Jeremy's old house and not at home with my mother and Vanessa. I jumped up and paced the floor, all the while, shaking my head as if the floor had an answer for me. I broke out into a cold sweat. Then, I heard *click, click+9 , click.* I stopped walking and turned away from any reflection of myself in the hopes that she would not appear. I started walking again as Nicole spoke to me, "Calm down, Nikki. Mother is dead. She can't hurt us anymore."

"Damn. It was just a dream," I said as I looked around the room.

"Yes Nikki. It was just a dream. Mother can't hurt us now."

With rage and a severe tone, I replied, "I thought I told you to leave me the fuck alone! I have a shit load of stuff on my mind. I will not rest until I am at peace."

"Nikki, I can't just do that. You are angry, and retaliation is on your mind."

"Nicole, you don't know the first thing about anger and retaliation."

"Nikki, I want you to be careful and listen. We can survive this ordeal."

"I guess being in Raymond Neil taught you that shit?" I asked her sarcastically.

"Being in Raymond Neil taught me that I am a winner and that I am somebody important, regardless of my outcome. Some are worse off than we are," Nicole said.

"I can't believe this shit. I'm standing here, talking to a reflection that does not have a damn clue about life. Yet, you're trying to school me with some group therapy shit. Fuck you!" I screamed at her.

In a despising tone, Nicole said, "Nikki, you are a monster."

She turned up her nose and continued by asking, "What have I created?"

Hearing those words caused me to stop completely. I searched her face as she spoke to me. I said quietly and calmly to the bitch that constantly got on my damn nerves, "I broke us out to kill Jeremy, and killing his ass is what I plan to do. He has to die like the rest of those fuckers did. Bitch, all I can tell you is to watch the fuck out because you can't stop me."

I stomped my feet on the floor and jumped up and down. I stopped abruptly, and then walked out of the bedroom and to the front door to see if anyone was outside. After observing my surroundings, I ran out of the house with only one thought on my mind— Find Jeremy.

Chapter 5

I got in the car and hit the road. While driving, I thought about Jeremy's aunt and uncle. They lived in Cedar City, Utah. It didn't matter how far I had to drive because I had to get the fuck out of Las Vegas. Everybody, including the police at Raymond Neal, was looking for me. It was funny though, because those bitches had caught me in Iuka, Mississippi and brought me all the way back to Las Vegas. As the doctor had put it, "You're in Nevada because you committed all those crimes here. There was no crime committed in Mississippi besides kidnapping Jeremy."

I was told, after the day Cowboy knocked me out, that his punk ass had called the Iuka Police Department in Mississippi. His monkey ass had tied me up until they got there. The Iuka PD had the BOLO come across their computer, so when Cowboy called me in, those country boys were all over my ass. The Iuka Police hauled my black ass off to jail and called the FBI. Within hours, the FBI came to pick me up and to lock me down in that mental institution. They boasted and shit like they'd captured me. I found out later that the FBI had a $50,000 dollar reward out for my arrest. Cowboy was a lucky

muther-fucker, but that was okay because once I laid eyes on him, I was going to peel his muther-fucking onion. All that shit crossed my mind as I drove to my destination.

I thought back to Jeremy. I knew he was close to his uncle. If anyone knew where he was, his Uncle Paul would know for sure. It was a long drive, but I was willing to take it. I was going to kill that muther-fucking Jeremy once I laid eyes on him, and he would regret the day he broke my heart.

I drove toward Utah for a couple of hours. I finally came down this country-ass dirt road once I made it into the state. Hogs were lying around in the sun, and about four cows had decided to cross the road as I approached.

I had to make a complete stop while waiting for the cows to pass. I looked over to my left. There was a small white house with black shutters right off the road. I let the windows down, trying to decide if that was Jeremy's aunt and uncle's house and was startled by a small cry. My heart began to race as the hairs stood up on the back of my neck. I looked over at a big-ass mailbox and realized there was a little girl sitting on the ground, crying the entire time, and I had never noticed. My first thought was to go to the girl because I remembered when Nicole used to cry all the time. I'd had to comfort her, so why not talk to this little girl and see what was going on. My head started ringing. *Click, click, click.*

"Drive the fuck off," I said as I second-guessed myself.

"Don't leave her Nikki. I know exactly how she feels," Nicole said.

"Damn bitch! I have another agenda. I can't sit around fucking off with this little pissy-ass girl. Suppose somebody comes out and sees me? Then, we're both fucked," I replied.

"Come on, Nikki. Nobody will see you. If that's the case, this little girl wouldn't be sitting out here, crying by herself, if she didn't think she was alone."

"Fuck it! You got a point," I replied to Nicole as I pulled onto the side of the road, got out, and approached the crying girl.

"Hey kid! What the hell is wrong with you?" I asked.

The child cried harder as she pointed towards the barn. I glanced at the barn, then looked back at the five or six-year-old child and asked, "What's going on in the barn?"

"My momma is hurting. I hear her screaming," she replied.

I looked toward the barn. I wasn't sure if I wanted to go over and find out what was going on, or leave this little girl here crying. Nicole kept trying to take over, wanting me to help this little muther-fucker.

Damn! Why can't I stay out of trouble? I wondered as I walked to the barn with the little girl. She had her hand over her mouth as we approached. I tried to figure out what the hell she was doing. *This kid is a little strange to me*, I thought.

As I got a little closer, I could hear noises. My mind began to wonder because the noises didn't sound like someone hurting. I motioned for the child to stay put and eased into the barn. I observed pitch forks, shovels, and hairy slaughtered pigs that were strung up by their heels in preparation for the large pot of boiling hot water that was also in the barn. I walked quietly around the big black pot, and I saw a woman that I assumed was the child's mother. She was saying, "Oh, yes! That feels so good."

I peeped around and saw that she was fucking somebody. I jumped back and was about to walk off until I noticed that that somebody was a young boy. He might have been twelve or thirteen. *This old ass muther-fucker is fucking a kid*, I thought as I watched the boy wipe off his dick with some sort of towel.

"Mrs. White, can I go now? I am tired, and you are working me too much today just for a ten speed mountain bike," the boy said.

"You have one more meeting with me before you get that bike. Besides, your folks know that you are here working. What? You don't like the work?" she asked the little boy in a sexy manner.

"I do, but I never thought I would be working like this. You said you wanted me to help you slaughter pigs, not have sex," he said, while putting on his pants and shoes.

"Come back tomorrow and I will throw in an extra fifty dollars," she said.

"Fifty dollars sounds good to me. I can do that," the boy said excitedly.

Before either one of them could leave the barn, I rushed back and told the little girl to go to her room inside the house. She looked up at me intensely before she turned and ran into the house. I didn't have time to make sure she went in because I had to hide quickly.

As I hid, I saw the teenager run to the back of the barn, by the woods, and walk down what looked like a trail. I couldn't believe this old-ass woman was seducing a kid. What the fuck was wrong with all these old muther-fuckers fucking kids? My blood began to boil like there was no tomorrow. This just reminded me of how my mother and father used to fuck me in the barn. My mother was rougher than my father. It was sad. They had both taken turns fucking their kids for completely different reasons. I grabbed my head as a pain hit me hard. *Click, click, click.* It hurt me so bad that I had to stand and stare at the wall to focus. My eye sight had disappeared there for a moment. The pains were hitting me so severely now. Ever since I had busted out of Raymond Neil, it had gotten worse.

When my vision returned, I continued to hide, so I could see what the old lady was going to do. I peeped around the corner and saw her still laying out on some hay, playing with her pussy. She was one of those horny, old muther-fuckers that couldn't get enough.

I came out into the open and closed the barn door. I picked up the pitch fork and walked over to her with no fear of what might happen.

"Who the hell are you and what the hell are you doing on my farm?" she yelled as she held her shirt up in front of her.

"What does it matter, bitch? I caught you fucking a young-ass boy. Who is he?" I asked.

"Get the fuck out of here!" she yelled as she tried to get up.

I lifted the pitch fork and stated, "If you get up, I will kill you."

She looked at me and fell back to the ground. "You are trespassing. Get your ass off my property now before I call the police," she demanded.

"Bitch, stop making idle threats before you really piss me off," I said.

"I'm calling the police," she said again as she jumped up and reached for a cell phone.

I ran up to her and stuck the pitch fork dead in her fucking chest, before she knew what had hit her. When I pulled it out, she fell to the ground. She tried to crawl away from me, but couldn't. I turned her over to face me and said, "Since you like kids, let me see you play with your pussy."

She looked at me with a stone face. Not a word came from her lips, only moaning sounds.

"Bitch, I don't want to hear you moan; I want to see some pussy popping or something," I said as I approached her.

She reached for me, and I kicked her under the neck. Screams rang from her mouth. To shut her up, I picked up the pitch fork and stabbed her in the throat. Blood oozed from her neck and out the corners of her mouth. I bent down between her legs. Her pussy lay exposed. I lifted one of her legs, and stuck one of my fingers in her and moved it in and out. She was very wet. That teenager must have nutted in her old ass. I looked up at her, and her eyes were wide open. I began finger fucking her with two fingers, then three, then four. Suddenly, her eyes blinked. *Damn, this bitch is still alive. She's a tough cookie,* I thought.

I bent both of her legs back and held them with my hands. She had a little hay stuck on her pussy, but I wanted to taste. I bent down and began licking her old ass pussy. Luckily, she had that shit shaved. I let her right leg go, and it flopped to the floor. I stuck two fingers in her pussy and continued tasting her. Once I saw her eyes close, I stopped. It was no fun if she wasn't looking.

I got up off the floor and said, "It's not good to rob children of their childhood. Take it from me. I am a prime example."

Her eyes were open wide, staring at me. I took the pitch fork from her neck, grabbed that old bitch by the hair and dragged her over to the pot of hot boiling water. Luckily for me, she wasn't that heavy. As she figured out where we were going, she kicked like a wild buck.

"Damn bitch! You still have a little fight in you," I said as I dumped her in head first.

She screamed and splashed all that fucking hot water on me. I let her go, and she fell to the ground, bucking and kicking. I grabbed her up by the hair again and pushed her entire body into the big black pot of boiling water. Then, I rushed to pick up the pitch fork to try to hold her down. This child-fucking bitch had to pay. I struggled, trying to keep that bitch under water. Every time she came up, she would scream. I thought, *Damn, I hope that little girl don't come out the house*. The thought passed quickly as I held that old bitch down longer and longer, until she slowly stopped moving.

Moments went by, and her struggling stopped completely. The boiling hot water was now bloody red, and the slaughter house no longer smelled of pigs, but of burnt human flesh. I threw the pitch fork down in the boiling hot water with the woman.

I stood there for a few minutes, looking at the dead woman. Then I realized the little girl was standing there. She

was holding her teddy bear, and tears were pouring down her face. I walked over to her and put my arms around her.

She asked, "Is Mommy dead?"

"Yes, bad people have to be punished, and she was being a bad girl. Are you a bad girl, too?" I asked, as the clicking began banging at my fucking head. *Click, click, click*.

"Don't fuck with me right now. Can't you see I am being the judge and jury here?" I said to Nicole.

"Don't kill this child. She has nothing to do with her mother. Please Nikki," Nicole said.

"I don't like to leave witnesses. Those muther-fuckers are like two-faced friends. To save their own ass, they'll give up yours."

"It does not matter. She is young and innocent. Don't kill her. Please, Nikki," Nicole begged.

"Bitch, did I ask you for any advice on what to do?" I retorted.

"Please Nikki, I'm begging you," Nicole implored.

The little girl looked up at me and said, "I want my mommy."

I looked over at the big pot boiling with pig, blood, bones and hair; I took the little girl over to her mother and spoke, "Do you want me to put you in this hot water?"

"No! No! I want my mommy," she screamed and cried.

"Get the fuck off me," I said as I pushed her down to the ground.

She fell to the ground screaming. I couldn't take all that fucking crying. It was bad enough that I had to hear Nicole cry all the time. I walked over and picked up a shovel. I rushed back over and picked the girl up and tossed her into the hot boiling water. I jumped back before any of it hit me. The girl tried to get out as she screamed, but I took the shovel and held her down. Her body touched the bottom, and within a minute, she was dead. I threw the shovel down to the ground and walked out of the barn. As I headed to my car, I took another look at the house, and there, standing in the window, was another little girl, staring directly at me.

"Don't Nikk! Let her be," Nicole said.

"You're right. Enough damage has been done here," I replied as I got into my car and drove off. This bullshit had already delayed me. I had to get the hell out of there and fast.

I drove and drove through the wee hours of the night until I finally arrived at Jeremy's Aunt Nancy and Uncle Paul's home. It was about six o'clock in the evening, and I knew they went to bed with the chickens. I made my way to their backyard storage, picked out the sharpest ax, touched the blade, and thought of the damage I could do. As the ax swung from my side, I made my way back to the house. I knew they had no alarm, so I found the spare key and let myself in. The house was clean, and as usual, the smell of apples and oranges filled my nostrils. I noticed flowers hanging everywhere as the dark room encumbered my vision. I went quietly to the living room and saw Uncle Paul. He was asleep and snoring. *How annoying*, I thought as I looked at him, with his head tilted in the soft gray recliner and unaware of my presence. I leaned closely to his ear and said softly, "Where is Jeremy?"

He mumbled inaudibly. Then, he said, "I don't know," as he turned his head.

I moved to the other side of his head and said "I will ask you once more. Where is Jeremy?"

He started waking up and responded, "Didn't I tell you that I didn't know?"

In a flash, I jumped in front of him and swung the ax as I said, "Wrong answer."

As his head rolled off of his neck and to the left, I looked at the headless body. I was amazed to see the blood spewing out the hole. I walked over to the head, picked it up and said, "You should have told me, and I would have let you live." I put the head back on the body, closed the eyes, shook my head and said, "Probably not."

I looked around to see if anyone else was present. Then I licked the ax, tore four strips off the curtain, and walked to the bedroom. Aunt Nancy was asleep, lying on her back in the middle of the small bed. I took one hand and tied it to the rail, but before I could tie up her other hand, she woke up.

I said, "If you move, I will kill you."

With fear gripping her heart, she became still and obeyed me. I tied up her other hand and both of her legs. Then, I climbed up and stood on the bed in front of her.

"Where is Jeremy?" I asked.

"Who are you?" she quizzed.

I showed her my ax and asked again, "Where is Jeremy?"

Her eyes were glued to my ax, but she didn't answer, so I raised it up and severed her knee from her leg. The blood gushed out as she cried out in pain.

"Now, Aunt Nancy, let us try this again. You know something, and if I have to bust your muther-fucking head to the white meat to get the answer out, I will. Now, since we have that out of the way, where the fuck is Jeremy?" I asked again.

She shook her head and cried as she replied, "Please, I don't know where he is. Don't hurt me anymore! Please don't hurt me!"

When she did not tell me what I wanted to know, I chopped down on her other knee and severed the knee from the leg. I glanced down at her legs, still tied to the bed, and saw blood everywhere. As she slipped into unconsciousness, her words became slurred.

"Bitch, you're making my job hard," I said.

Somehow, she got the courage to say to me, "I would never tell you where he is. Even if I did know, I'd take it to the grave."

"You never liked me anyway, and how funny you would say that," I replied.

I started swinging out of control until I was out of breath. I sat down on the edge of the bed and looked back over my right shoulder at Aunt Nancy. She was unrecognizable. Body parts and flesh were all over the small, bloody bed, but her limbs were still tied up and dangling.

Memories of Jeremy came to mind, so I sat on the bed, lost in reverie. I closed my eyes as I became further engrossed in thought.

He was holding my hand as we talked about our life together. He discussed with me happy memories in his life and how he looked forward to marrying his best friend. I looked at him and smiled happily. He took his fingers and brushed the hair out of my face. Then, he used the back of his hand and traced my face as his hand cupped my chin. One finger of his other hand went between the depths of my breasts and rubbed a nipple.

I moved my head to the right. I opened my eyes and realized that now, more than ever, I needed to find him.

I rolled Aunt Nancy up in the bed sheets, rolled her off the bed and laid back on the bed.

A few moments later, I got up because my stomach growled, and I noticed where I was laying. I went over to the closet to find a new outfit. I had to improvise because her clothing was a little bigger than my size. I walked to the bathroom with the clothes, placed them on the toilet lid and took a shower. As the water splashed in my face, I realized that I had never felt so alive and alert. It was because I knew Jeremy would be mine soon. *I can literally taste his blood,* I thought as the water tried to cleanse me.

I stepped out of the shower, dried off and put on Aunt Nancy's clothes. Seeing myself in the mirror was inevitable, so I looked up and faced my reflection in the mirror.

The clicking was louder, and I tried to make it stop by hitting my head against the wall. "Make it stop! Make it stop!" I yelled. Then, I got tired and sat down in front of the mirror.

"There you go again, killing more people," Nicole accused, then turned her back.

Without saying a word, I smashed the mirror and walked back to the bedroom. I noticed a gun cabinet and opened it up with the key that was stuck in the knob. I took the 9mm, but it had no bullets. I looked around until I found a box of 9mm bullets. I gathered the gun and bullets, sat on the bed, and loaded the gun slowly. After making sure one was in the chamber, I pointed it and thought, *This muther-fucker is ready to rock and roll.*

I got up and looked down at Aunt Nancy's body. I could not resist, so I said, "Aunt Nancy, you need to go and clean yourself up."

I smiled as I threw my towel on her bloody, sheet covered body.

I went to the kitchen and opened the fridge, but I did not see anything I really wanted, so I fixed a bowl of cereal.

"Just my damn luck— Bran flakes," I said as I ate the bowl of cereal and covered Paul up with a blanket that was next to him.

I looked through all of their mail, but nothing was there from Jeremy. I searched their important numbers that were in the back of the phone book, but no number for Jeremy.

"I know damn well they have a number or something for him," I said as I continued to search the house up and down, in and out. Nothing gave me a clue. It seemed that Jeremy had never been there or that they had ever contacted him. It was like he'd disappeared, but, one thing I knew about magicians, they had to reappear somewhere else.

Angry and discouraged, because this stop was also a bust, I suddenly felt exhausted from all the rambling around. I walked over to Uncle Paul's dead body and said, "Do you mind if I rest here for a spell? Thanks."

I got the other pillow and blanket that were lying by Jeremy's Uncle Paul, stretched out on the short couch, next to the closet, just in case I needed a quick getaway, and settled down for a long-awaited rest. It would soon be daylight, and I needed the rest.

CHAPTER 6

As I dozed off to sleep on the short couch in Jeremy's uncle and aunt's house, my dreams were of Jeremy until the *click, click, click* noises became very intense. Damn, this bitch was invading my dreams.

"Well, well, well. We finally meet up, Nicole," I said as we looked at each other from head to toe.

"Nikki, you have gone too far with all this killing. It has to stop now," Nicole said.

"And what if it doesn't? Do you have a plan that I don't know about?" I replied.

"You will grieve the day you ever took over my life," Nicole threatened.

"You can't be serious. To kill me is to kill you. Are you ready to go to hell?" I asked.

"I'm ready to go any day, as long as I can put a stop to a murderous person like you," Nicole said without blinking her eyes or moving.

"I'm going to have to watch you, bitch. I believe the saying now that you can be your own worst enemy. Every time I look

around, you become a thorn in my side. Don't make me pluck that rose," I said as evil gleamed all over me.

"At first, I wanted everyone that had ever wronged me dead, but, after being away for a while, I have come to view life differently," Nicole said.

"Bitch, that's you! I am out here, and you are in there," I said as I pointed to my head.

"I have no idea how you became so cruel and evil hearted," Nicole said to me.

"You don't have any idea? Let me refresh your memory. 'If I had a best friend, her name would be Nikki'."

"Shut up! I was a lonely child. I don't remember asking for a psychopath to replace me," Nicole said.

I laughed at her and responded, "We never get what the fuck we want, now, do we?"

"I love you, Nikki, and I hate you at the same time," Nicole said as tears streamed down her face.

"See, bitch? You are crying. How in the hell would you have ever been able to pull the shit off that I do with muther-fucking tears in your eyes? Cash those damn tears in for somebody's blood. My bad. The only muther-fucker you ever tried to hurt was me, right? The only muther-fucking one that has your back, and now you're trying to take me out the game? Nicole, now that is fucked up," I said to her.

She dried her tears and responded, "You don't think I can function where you are? You don't think I can do better about my life and feelings? If I'm trying to stop you, it's because I'm trying to help you help me."

I looked at her closely and said, "I don't need your damn help, my level is too advanced for your dumb ass."

When I walked off, a sharp pain hit me hard. I turned around and saw that Nicole had stabbed me in the lower left part of my back with her right hand. Before my mind came to terms with the fact that my best friend had stabbed me in the back, Nicole started stabbing and cutting me with so much force that all I could do was fall, face first, where I was, and she did not show me any mercy. I never thought she would come back like that, but she did. So many times, I'd called her out, saying she was weak and couldn't do the damn thing; however, here she was showing me.

Suddenly, I heard the sound of a man's voice coming through my sleep. I jumped up and looked for stab wounds and slices, but did not see any. I took my left hand and wiped my face because that dream had felt so damn real. It was at that moment that I knew that if I slipped, that bitch Nicole would get the drop on me and reclaim her life. I shook my head. I knew that bullshit was not going to happen; I wouldn't let it.

I remembered that I'd heard a man's voice, so I jumped up and ran to the living room closet before anyone saw me. I had to leave it cracked to see, although I didn't want to risk being heard. Luckily, I had this getaway plan to dash to the closet and hide before I got caught. I peeped through the crack and saw a short, stocky man come in the back door with keys in his hand. I looked closely at him and realized it was Isaac, Jeremy's worrisome cousin. He didn't like me, and I didn't like him. He put the keys in his pocket as he walked farther into the kitchen. He looked in the cabinet and got two bowls and two spoons down. He opened the fridge door and looked in. Walking towards Uncle Paul was a little boy around the age of six. When he took off his baseball cap, I recognized him to be Isaac's son, Isaiah. He walked back over to his father and whispered loudly, "Daddy, is Grandpa asleep?"

"Hush, don't wake him up. It's not like him to be sleeping this time of day, though. Let us eat something before we bother him, okay, son?"

"Okay Dad."

Isaiah walked to the other side of the kitchen and sat at the table with his father as a bowl of cereal was placed before him.

"Dad, I am glad you are my dad," Isaiah said between bites of cereal.

As he sat in front of his son, Isaac replied, "Isaiah, it is an honor to be your father."

Isaac started munching down on the cereal. His son, then said, "When are you going to tell me about the birds and the bees, Daddy?"

Nearly choking, Isaac replied, "Where'd you get that from?" The sounds of spoons hitting the glass bowls could be heard in the silent house.

"A boy on my peewee team said that his dad told him and his brother about a bird and a bee," Isaiah replied.

"A bird and a bee?" Isaac asked, trying to humor his son.

"Yeah. His brother likes a girl, and he said his dad said that he was only going to have the talk one time. Sam listened and told me to ask you. Sam then said his dad said that every boy needs to hear the bird and bee story."

Laughing at his son, Isaac smiled and then replied, "The bird and bee story. Isaiah, when you get old enough, I promise to have the bird and bee talk with you, but for now, eat your cereal." To humor his son more, Isaac said, "And bee quiet."

They laughed about that, then Isaac shushed him and said, "Isaiah, we don't want to bother your grandma and grandpa, do we?"

"No we don't, but you promise to tell me one day?" Isaiah asked his father as he slurped his bowl clean.

As he looked at his son's innocent face, Isaac replied with joy, "I will my son, I will."

Isaiah got up from the table, walked toward his grandpa and said, "Wake up."

His grandfather Paul did not respond. This time, Isaiah gently touched Paul and said, "Grandpa, it's time to wake up."

Suddenly, Paul's head rolled to the floor with a thump. The little boy screamed hysterically. Isaac hurried to the living room and the sight left him speechless. He ran over to his father's lifeless body and fell to his knees out of breath, for the sight was too much for him to endure. His son, on the other hand, was frozen, and neither one of them saw me come out of the closet. With my 9mm aimed, I harshly demanded, "Shut the fuck up!" They both looked up, startled and confused. When Isaac looked up and saw me standing there, in a raspy tone, he stammered, "Y-y-you did this?"

"I ask the questions, not you," I said with my gun aimed at Isaiah's head. "Where is Jeremy?"

"I haven't seen him in months. Please don't hurt my son. I told you all I knew," Isaac replied.

"I get tired of people trying to tell me what the fuck to do. Before I do anything stupid, tell me where the hell is your cousin?"

Isaac did not say a word, so I shot Isaiah in the leg. The boy screamed as he cried from the pain of the gunshot wound. Isaac began begging me as he focused on his son screaming.

"Alright,! Alright, you crazy bitch! I'll tell you where he is, if you let my son go," Isaac said.

As I looked at the worthless bastard begging like a fool, I lowered the gun, picked up Isaiah and threw him on the couch as he cried. I returned my attention back to Isaac and asked again, "Where did you say Jeremy is?"

"I heard he lives somewhere in Nevada, but I'm not sure where," he answered.

"What do you mean that you are not sure where?" I asked.

Isaac was trying to get off his knees as he talked, "I really don't have a clue."

"Is Jeremy your cousin?" I asked. He looked confused about the question, but he answered, "Yes."

"Is that your son on the couch?" I asked, and he looked confused about that question. I pointed the gun at Isaiah.

He answered, "Yes, that's my son, whom I love dearly."

"You answered those questions, but you can't tell me where the fuck your cousin is?" I spat.

Isaiah began crying, and my focus went to him as he whined, "Daddy, help me!"

"It's going to be okay, son. Hang in there," Isaac reassured him.

I continued to watch Isaiah, but, out of the corner of my eye, I saw that Isaac was trying to rush me. Without hesitation, I shot Isaiah in the other leg. Isaac fell back to his knees and yelled, "I'm sorry! I'm fucking sorry! Please don't shoot my son anymore! That's my little boy, my angel!"

"Don't worry. It'll be okay, Daddy. He'll be God's angel now," I replied.

I looked Isaac in the eyes. Then, I turned and aimed my 9mm at Isaiah. With one direct shot, a bullet penetrated his head. A father's rage caused Isaac to come at me. He did not make it close to me. I reacted by shooting him multiple times in the chest. As he lay there, trembling, I said, "Silly bastard, you should have told your son about the birds and the bees today."

Then, I shot him once in the head. I turned him over, looking for money and his car keys.

I took the car keys from his pocket and kicked him as I walked out the door.

I went back to the nurse's car and placed it in Nancy and Paul's garage. I scoped the garage out, picked up a shovel and two knives, and placed them in Isaac's car, along with the 9mm. I shut the door and went back to the house to look around for more items. My first thought was to burn the house down because, fingerprints or no fingerprints, I couldn't risk getting caught. I saw nothing in the kitchen, so I went to the living room, and there, I noticed an air freshener can. I went back into the kitchen and turned on the gas stove top. After placing the can in the microwave, I closed the door and went to Isaac's car. When I looked in my rearview mirror, the clicking began as the house went up in flames. *Click, click, click.* I turned my head, then looked back into the mirror again. That fake-ass Nicole was staring at me and looked like she had some bullshit to say, as she did whenever I did something. I glanced at Nicole in the mirror and asked, "Bitch, what the hell you want now?"

"Nikki, a little boy? Jeremy is not worth you killing a child. I tell you this every day," she reprimanded.

"And I tell you this every day. Shut the fuck up. The little boy was in the right place at the wrong time. So, what the hell did you want me to do? Have him rat me out, or better yet, help his daddy tie me up, so I could go back to that boring-ass RNPI?"

"Nikki, you didn't have to do it. You know how I feel about killing, and to have a child die at my hands is heart-wrecking."

"Bitch, you mean to die at my hands because I am the one on the outside," I said to her casually.

"Your hands, my hands. Innocent people still die," Nicole said.

"When are you ever going to have something to say that I want to hear? You know what? Shut the fuck up talking to me, until you can say something productive," I said.

I sat there for a few minutes, trying to figure which way to go since night had fallen. I couldn't believe that I'd driven all the way to Cedar City, Utah, thinking Jeremy would be there. Now, I had to travel back to Nevada and risk getting busted. Fuck it! I would find Jeremy and kill him. If the police tried to stop me, then we all would die, but Jeremy Bland would die this year. Silence filled the air as Nicole and I rode to the next town and gassed up the car.

CHAPTER 7

Many hours passed, and Nicole hadn't clicked in my head yet. *The bitch must be asleep*, I thought. Cars were passing me and some even honked their horns at me. *This must be a damn popular car. Then again, Isaac was a well-known whore*, I thought as I drove a little faster.

"I've got to lay my ass low for a couple of days, but I have no idea where."

I had to be careful of not being seen and shit. I knew those pigs were probably looking for me everywhere. I drove around a little longer until the idea hit me. I thought about Jake. I heard he'd moved to Garrison, Utah, and I was sure he wouldn't mind if he had an old friend drop by. He and I had grown up together. I had only seen him a few times since we'd become adults, but I considered him a friend. He had been in prison for fifteen years for raping and sodomizing a woman. He had a few screws loose, but the court said he was sane enough to stand trial. I knew he was fucked up because, when I had shot Vanessa, he'd still fucked her while blood was pouring out her body. I continued driving for a few minutes and had a flash back. *Jake made Vanessa suck his dick while she bled out. I guess she was slow, so he shoved her back down onto the floor.*

He flipped her over and began fucking her in the ass too. He was pounding hard against her body. He was fucking like a nigga just got out of jail.

"My bad, he had just gotten out of jail," I said out loud and laughed.

All you could hear was dick slapping against ass and screams of pain filling the air.

He was a crazy-ass muther-fucker, but a friend I could halfway trust. I shook my head, and I flashed back to reality.

I took a left exit and drove slowly because I did not need to miss the county line road. I hadn't been there in a while, but I knew I would know it when I saw it. I drove a little further on the road, but I saw nothing. I was about to turn around, but then I saw a sign that read TREETOP TRAILER PARK. I smiled to myself, because I knew no one would ever connect me to Jake. I drove the loud colored car into the trailer park. I looked around but did not see his trailer at first, but when I saw his old car, I knew I had found him at last.

When I pulled up, he was looking out the door. I got out and with surprise, he said, "If you aren't a sight for sore eyes, my yellow rose of Texas. What wind storm has blown you this way?"

"I'm in need of a little rest and relaxation. Think you can help a girl out?" I asked.

"Sure can. Come on in and take a load off," he replied.

Jake and I walked into the trailer arm in arm like old partners who hadn't seen each other in years. As I walked further into the trailer and looked around, I noticed right away that Jake had been up to his old tricks again. The inside of the mobile home had beer cans and cigarette butts scattered everywhere, and the stink was horrible.

Jake only looked like a pure slob when he was hired to do some dirty work. Because the job had him busy, the mobile home went untidy. I just stood there because I really did not want to sit down. Nevertheless, to stay the night and eat in that nasty muther-fucker was the best I could do. Jake came up behind me and said, “Grab a seat. You thirsty for some beer or vodka? Are you hungry?”

I looked around that nasty bitch.

“I’ll be damned if I eat here,” I said to myself, but to Jake, I just declined the food quickly and settled for a cold beer and vodka. He took a swallow of his beer and nearly knocked his can out before asking, “What the fuck are you into now, Nicole?”

“Why you say that shit for?” I asked.

In his country twang voice, he replied, “You are here, and you didn’t come here just for a damn social call. So, what the fuck is going on?”

“I left the damn institute. I broke out that bitch,” I answered as I opened my beer.

“Hell yeah! That’s the shit I’m talking about. Don’t let any damn body tell you what you can and can’t do. Make those fuckers search for you, and you do know they’re looking for your black ass, right?”

He lifted up his can of beer to mine. We laughed as we toasted to the shit he had just said.

“Here nigga. Here. Try this shit,” Jake said as he handed me a white pill.

I put the pill in my mouth and closed my eyes. Soon, I began to feel strange, but it was a good strange.

"What is that shit?" I asked him as I drank more beer.

"That little pill you took? Oh, that's called the Mr. Muther Fucker because it will make you do, hear, and say any muther-fucking thing you need it to," Jake laughed.

Click, click, click. I stood up and screamed before I fell back on the couch.

"Bitch, can't you see that I am having a damn good time? You're always showing up when shit is going good for me," I said.

Jake screamed out very loudly and said as he laughed; "Now bitch, that's that Mr. Muther Fucker right there. I told you that Mr. Muther Fucker was off the chain. You will see some shit," he continued.

"Nikki, can we go?" Nicole asked.

"I am enjoying myself. Aren't you?" I yelled to Nicole.

"I look tired and drunk, Nikki. Let us lie down and sober up some first, before you party more," Nicole said.

"You may look tired, but I'm drunk. Take your tired ass to bed," I said. As I laughed, I said loudly, "You can't go to bed until I go to bed. Now, ain't that a bitch? Guess what tho'? I ain't tired, and I ain't sleepy." I took a few more pills and watched Jake laugh.

"Every time you don't listen to me, things happen. I end up being right," Nicole replied.

"Maybe so, but I plan to enjoy my life, and I will enjoy this day with my partner-in-crime Jake," I said as I raised my vodka glass and toasted Jake. He laughed at me.

"Girl, tell that bitch in your head to step the fuck off before we off her ass too. Grown folks partying over here. No imaginary friends allowed," Jake said as he laughed harder.

"Alright bitch, you heard him. Make your ass like a ball and bounce before I play soccer," I said as I continued partying with Jake.

"Watch this before I go," Nicole said.

Nicole began making my body move like I was having a seizure. I started jerking and knocking all of Jake's stuff over. I began hitting myself and squeezing my breasts. Jake laughed as Nicole continued to make me look stupid. She made my hands hit my head and made me dance like a wild woman. When she was finished with her little game, she threw my body on the couch.

"See! You don't have complete control over me, just enough to keep me down," Nicole said in my mind and left. She was right, but for now, she could be.

"Man, that was some freaky shit! What did you take, so I can take it?" Jake asked.

"Check this out. This is my personal bowl of Skittles. Reach in and get some of the rainbow," he said as we both laughed because that shit was damn funny.

"Nicole, take this. Here is a little something extra to help you get the edge off while you are here," he continued.

I took the light blue pill from Jake's hand. I placed it in my mouth and closed my eyes. This pill was nothing like the last one I'd had. This light blue pill made me become hyper. My senses became keen and there seemed to be nothing I couldn't do. Jake put on some music, and I began dancing. It felt wonderful to let loose and feel free. The music did something to me, and everything was happening fast, so I sat down. I looked up and a man was with Jake. He sat down close to me and put his arm around me.

"What's up? I'm Eric."

"I'm Nikki. What you want to do?"

"After we drink, we can fuck," he said bluntly.

I got up, twirled around in circles and then said, "Get a few more drinks in you, and we can go from there. That's if you're up to it?"

"Girl, I'm up for anything," he said as he drank more beer.

"Got any weed on you?" I asked, already high as a kite.

He lit up the stanky shit, and it smelled good. I looked over at Eric, and he was opening up a beer and drinking twenty ounces down fast. The more he drank, the more pills I took.

"Jake, you know how to throw your girl a welcome home party," I said as I grinded on Eric.

"Hell bitch! This ain't shit. If I'd have known you were coming, I would have had it set out for sure," he said as he passed out.

Eric kissed me. His wet kisses reminded me of a puppy licking my face, but I was high, and he was the closest piece I had had in a while. So, I thought, *Why the fuck not?* His rough demeanor was alluring, and I loved it. He wasn't all that bad looking, but surely no Jeremy. Eric wanted to take me right there, but I needed a little more privacy. I took one good look at him, grabbed him by the hand and led him to the bedroom down the hall by the bathroom. I giggled as he threw me on the bed. I laid back and watched him take off his clothes.

Realizing that I was about to give him free sex, he helped me take off my clothes. He eyed my body up and down, got on top of me, and entered me hard. His dick was not that big, and he was heavy because many drunken men don't perform well; also, his strokes were nothing like my Jeremy or that of any man for that matter, but I needed to release all the same. I closed my eyes and pretended he was my love that was pleasing me. Somewhere along the way, that worked; my nut was outrageously good because of the thoughts I had of Jeremy. Eric stroked me a few times, then took out his dick and nutted all over my stomach.

Eric fell on top of me, breathing hard. He fell asleep immediately. I took his weight as long as I could, then I pushed him off me. He made a few more noises, but he was asleep. I laid there for almost an hour, just yearning for the touch of Jeremy. I finally made up my mind to go eat, and I started getting up. When I made it to Eric's side of the bed, I fell, and he woke up. He glanced at me with surprise, then he asked, "Are you stealing, bitch?"

I was stunned by the question, but I replied, "Hell no! I fell, muther-fucker. If I were stealing from you, you'd be dead."

I got up from the floor and gave Eric a stare that said, I don't play bullshit games with any muther-fucker.

He stared back and said, "Why in the hell is my wallet on the floor in front of you?"

I looked down, and there his wallet was. If I didn't know better, it would look like I was stealing, but I know me. I don't steal from the living. I looked at him again and replied angrily, "I don't know! I told you. I fell!"

He came closer to me and grabbed me with his left hand. Using his bad boy tone he said, "I refuse to let a bitch steal from me."

"Let me go. I told you I was not stealing. I fell down, and you woke up. Now let me go!" I yelled.

He reached over and slapped me so hard that I fell to my knees. He picked me up and threw me on the bed. I struggled with him and did not make it easy for him to attack me. He got on the bed and straddled me. In a move I had never seen before, Eric placed his arms under my neck and started choking me.

"Since you wanna steal from me, I'm gonna teach you a lesson," he said while pulling out his dick and stuffing it in my pussy. It burned and hurt, and I knew my walls were raw. He choked me harder and harder as he pounded my pussy harder and harder. My eyes rolled into the back of my head, and my screams felt empty, so I just stopped. I heard Jake screaming in the background, telling Eric to get off me. I glanced over and saw Jake rush Eric. He finally got him off me, and I sat up gasping for air. Jake and Eric were rolling around on the floor as I got up and snatched my gun from my bag. I pointed it at Eric and yelled, "Stop, Eric, or I'll shoot!"

With frantic breathing, they continued to wrestle. I stumbled over some clothes, got up close and personal to Eric's head, and pulled the trigger. The crackling of the shot made Jake shake. He looked at me with a look that my sister used to give me, whenever I did something wrong.

"You shot him. You bitch, you didn't have to shoot him!" Jake yelled at me with a temper."

"I was helping you!" I screamed back at him, but he just looked at me and replied,

"You didn't have to kill him. He was having a little fun. That's all," he said as he came closer to me.

"Stay away from me Jake," I said as I pointed the gun at him.

"What you going to do? Shoot me too, like you did your momma?" Jake teased me.

"Shut the fuck up Jake, because you don't want this issue with me," I warned.

While walking closer to me, he said, "You won't shoot me, will you bitch?"

"No muther-fucker, but you better step back and stop bullshitting," I said as I lowered the gun.

"Damn bitch! I really thought you were going to shoot me," Jake replied.

"Hell no! We have been through too fucking much," I answered.

"You got that shit right," he said.

I bent over coughing, with my hands on my knees. Jake rushed over and began patting me on the back. I stood straight up, and felt under my neck as I looked over at Eric's dead body.

"Damn Jake! That nigga almost killed me. Lucky you did come in and save me," I said while still rubbing my neck.

"That's what friends are for. Now, I need a little pay back, don't you think?" he replied.

"What?" I said, surprised.

"Yeah bitch, you owe me. You know I've wanted to fuck you every since we were small," he said.

"Yeah nigga, but I thought you were full of shit," I replied as my mind began to wonder if I should fuck this nigga or not.

"Come on. Give me a taste of that mean-ass pussy you got; you know the word was that shit was invincible," he laughed.

"Cool. I'll give you this pussy, but you have got to hurry up. I've spent too much time fucking off, and the cops might come around this bitch looking for me."

"Shit girl! We need to get to fucking then," he said.

After I gathered my clothes, Jake and I walked out of the room and to his room. That fucking room was so junky that I was surprised rats wasn't in that bitch. I placed the gun on Jake's night stand, laid on the bed and spread my legs wide. Jake dived down on me, licking my clit and slurping like it was an ice cream cone.

"Get up nigga! I don't have all night for you to eat my pussy. Fuck me, so I can go," I demanded.

"Sounds good to me," he replied.

Jake crawled on top of me and began fucking immediately. He had a big horse dick. I was scared at first, but took it like a champion. He stroked and stroked; then I realized that this nigga didn't put on a rubber. Fuck it; I didn't fuck Eric with a rubber either. I hoped these bitches didn't have that kind of disease.

Jake fucked me for about fifteen minutes before he busted his nut. I pretended not to like it, but he really knew what the hell he was doing. He had moved around and around, up and down. He stroked hard, and he stroked soft. I had to give him credit; he knew how to fuck with that big-ass dingaling, but that was not where my heart was. After Jake rolled over, he said, "Damn, you got some bomb-ass pussy. Wish I would have fucked you when we were younger. If I had known it was that good, I would have held you down and took that fucking pussy."

Click, click, click. My fucking head went to banging. This bitch said he would have held me down and fucked me. He would have raped me. My mind flipped out, and I got up.

"You're a dirty muther-fucker Jake. You would have raped me? Is that what you're saying?" I asked him, as I stood next to the small night stand he had.

"Naw bitch! I would have asked first, then took the pussy," he answered while laughing.

"Glad to know that, you dirty bastard," I replied as I rushed to pick up the gun on the night stand and killed that muther-fucker where he laid. I poured six bullets into his body. He jerked like he was having a seizure.

I got on the bed, looked down at Jake's body and said, "Never underestimate what a killer will or won't do. You should know. You taught me that," I said as I picked his pocket clean.

I made my way to the kitchen and tried to find something, anything to help me destroy this piece of shit trailer he called a home. I opened up cabinets, but did not find anything of use, until I saw the rubbing alcohol. I threw it around the dump, picked up a lighter and threw it on the trail of alcohol. That did not do; therefore, I turned on the gas stove and placed a bottle of fly spray in the microwave. I decided not to wait nearby, so I left the trailer and went a little further down the street, while waiting on a smoke scene. *Click, click, click*.

"Nikki, let me out! I know you hear me!" Nicole screamed.

I ignored her until she said, "If you feel what you are doing is so right, then why did you run, Nikki?"

When I looked at her, she smirked and looked as if she was posing for the camera.

I replied, "You think you are so damn perfect, don't you, Nicole?"

"I am only as good as you make me, Nikki; and that is not that good at all," she shot back.

I had grown very tired of talking to Nicole. It had gotten to the point where her voice was really beginning to irritate me. This fucking whining and crying about every fucking thing that I did was messing with my head. This bitch wasn't on my team anymore. She said that she was down for me, but I couldn't tell. When I got in the car, I looked into the rearview to see Nicole looking like a fucking jackass, so I bashed the rearview mirror to pieces until it fell off. That way I didn't have to worry about that bitch getting on my last nerve. I couldn't focus on Jeremy, because this bitch was in my ear, talking out the side of her fucking neck.

"Fuck you Nicole," I said as I turned around and saw black smoke pouring out from the roof of the trailer. I began to drive and headed for Ely, Nevada.

Chapter 8

As I headed for Ely, thoughts of me killing Marvin flashed in my head. That nigga was the love of my life. I'd given him racks and racks of cash, bought flashy cars for his black ass, and when we first began dating, I'd watched him fuck another bitch. That was how deep I loved that nigga. Eventually, I took all I could and decided to decapitate that muther-fucker. *I wonder how he feels now*, I thought as I laughed out loud.

"Bitch, we fucked that nigga up. I bet he won't talk shit to you now," I boasted.

"Yes you did, Nikki. We did," Nicole said soberly.

"Don't get mushy on me now Nicole. I'm so tired of the fucking crying and moping that you do all day long. We have talked about living our life to the fullest, and here you are daydreaming about a nigga who is dead," I spoke with anger and resentment.

"Why are you mad at me, Nikki? It's definitely not my fault that you've gone crazy," Nicole replied.

"Crazy? I'm beyond that. I'm fucking deranged about all this bull shit you're letting happen to you. I came into your life to protect you. You seem to be forgetting that shit. I am here for you. Believe that shit because it is real."

"How can I forget Nikki? You remind me every day," Nicole replied.

"Like you remind me every day to stop doing the shit I do, but the shit I do gets me through," I said.

"Well, stop reminding me that I was weak," Nicole said to me.

"I remind you so that you can keep your mind on track. I fucking love you girl. That's why I do the shit I do. I know you fucking love me because if you didn't, I wouldn't mutherfucking be here now," I said to Nicole.

"I love you too Nikki, but sometimes you go too far. Protect me; don't kill for me," Nicole said with tears in her eyes.

"Bitch, don't start that crying shit. I get tired of seeing water fall from your damn eyes. Dry that shit up," I demanded as I drove down the highway.

"I'm not going to cry. Sometimes, I just feel very emotional," Nicole replied.

"I don't give a fuck about your emotions. Get it together bitch," I answered.

"I thought you cared about me and my emotions," Nicole said sadly.

"On the real tip? Hell no! I don't care about how you feel anymore. You seem to have forgotten that we killed all those muther-fuckers together. You acting like I did this by myself. The way the world looks at it, I'm in your damn mind and not the other way around. Bitch, they don't see me; they see you."

"This was your idea since day one, to keep me down and eventually take over, wasn't it?" Nicole spoke up.

"Really Nicole? My idea? Well, that may be true, but you started depending on me more when Jeremy came into the picture. Besides, that is who you love, isn't it? I don't love that nigga. Frankly, I don't give a fuck if he lives or dies," I said.

"Nikki, you have to love him. You did sleep with him," Nicole pointed out.

"Bitch, it's a difference between fuck and sleep. I fucked him. Don't get it twisted," I retorted.

My first thought was to curse this muther-fucker out and be done with it, but I missed talking to her at times, and she needed me to protect her from whore-ass niggas like Marvin and Jeremy.

As I continued to drive, I thought about Marvin. His death played in my head like a movie. My mind went back to when I walked up to him as his head was down while he counted money. *Before he could turn around and say anything else, I stabbed that muther-fucker in the right side of his neck with one knife. Then, I stabbed him again on the left side of his neck with another knife. His whole body froze, stiff like a hard dick ready to fuck. I pushed the knives deeper into his neck. Hot blood spurted out as I tried to take his head off, as I pushed deeper and deeper. He reached out. I realized he was going for his gun that was sitting on the table. I released the knives and grabbed the gun. His body went limp like an impotent muther-fucker.*

As I drove, I tried to erase the memory from my head, but I couldn't help but to think on it. In a way, the memory encouraged me to go out and fuck up more people. The feeling was unexplainable. My heart was broken, and my feelings were hurt. That bitch played with my heart, and it cost him his life. Fuck that pussy-ass nigga.

I continued to reminisce. *I pushed the chair to the floor while his body fell helplessly. He laid there, shaking like the pussy he was. We stared at each other. I stared into his eyes, trying to see his love for me, but his heart was so cold. I remember bending down, pushing my knives forward and slicing open his neck. Blood squirted everywhere as he placed his hands over his wound. I placed the knives on the table and racked his gun back to put a bullet in the chamber. It felt good to have him on this side of the fence. Now, he could see how it felt to be down like a weak-ass muther-fucker. There were plenty of nights he had beaten me and left me looking stupid in the face.*

He laid on the floor, gasping for air. Blood was running down both corners of his mouth. I pointed the gun as he continued to stare up at me. I aimed it at his legs and released two bullets, one in each leg.

"This is for all the pussy niggas around the world fucking over women and using them," I said. As I poured two more bullets into his fat-ass stomach, I said, "This is for all the pain and hurt you put into my heart."

Two more bullets violated his body, went straight into his chest.

"This is because I loved you unconditionally," I concluded.

I shook my head as those thoughts poured into my head. To think back, it brought tears to my eyes. I'd really loved that nigga, but he didn't give a fuck about me. No other woman would have cared for and loved him the way I did. What the fuck was wrong with that nigga? I pulled over to the side of the street as I began to cry. The tears were full blown, running down my face. Then, those damn clicking noise began. *Click, click, click*.

As I became consumed with anger, I banged and banged on the steering wheel. I kept beating and beating until I hit too hard and hurt my hand.

"Bitch, he's dead now," I yelled at Nicole.

"I know he's dead. You killed the love of my life," I replied.

"You need to get real. That nigga didn't love you. He only loved what you could give to him and do for him. Don't be such a dumb bitch," Nikki said venomously.

"Stop calling me a dumb bitch. I have more sense than you. I'm not the one going around killing people. You are really getting out of control."

"Fuck you Nicole. One day, I will get rid of you."

"Nikki, if I go down, we both go down."

I stepped on the gas and drove like a wild muther-fucker. Nicole had really pissed me off with all this crying. *When is this fake ass bitch going to grow up?* I wondered. She meant the world to me, but I hated the fact that she cried and whined like a fucking baby. It made me sad because I loved Nicole. I was here to love and protect her, not bring her down, but it seemed like she tried to bring me down with all this crying and shit. This bitch was about to make me get ignorant on her.

"Damn Nicole, I'm sorry for hurting your feelings, but you get on my fucking nerves when I feel like you aren't on my side. We are in this together, and you acting all soft. What's up with that?" I asked her.

"Nothing is up. I think all this shit is beginning to get a little too wild for me," Nicole answered.

"I'm not holding you against your will. If you don't want to do this, then get the fuck out," I yelled as I jammed on the brakes in the middle of the street.

"No Nikki. I'm not getting out. We are together as one," Nicole said.

"Well, act like it, bitch. I thought you were my ride-or-die bitch," I said.

"I am Nikki."

"Cool. Then, shut the fuck up and ride," I demanded as I took off, wheeling the tires on the highway.

I let my mind go back to how I'd killed Marvin's pussy ass. *I remembered how his body slowly relaxed as blood continued to ooze out of his mouth. I looked at him with no remorse, just pure hatred. It actually felt good to release all the anger and hurt he'd caused me on a daily basis. As his body laid on the floor, a flash back hit me of when he'd pissed in my face earlier that day. He'd taken out his fucking dick and literally pissed on me like I was nothing. A dead dog was treated better than I had been treated that day.*

A smile came over my face as I remembered pulling down my thong and bending down over his face. I opened his mouth, and I pissed straight into his muther-fucking mouth. As I pissed on his face and in his mouth, it mixed with blood, filled up his mouth and rolled out of the corner of his mouth. I wanted to defecate in his mouth, but I decided that my feces was too good for his no good pussy ass. All I could see were his eyes staring up at the ceiling. He was dead as a muther-fucking door knob.

As I snapped back to the present, I laughed out loud and said, "Damn, I fucked that pussy nigga up."

Chapter 9

The flashing of blue and red lights helped bring my trip down memory lane to an end. I began to pull over, so the pig would go by, but he was coming up behind me. I waited until he got out the car, then I sped off on the uphill dusty road. *Click, click, click*. Those fucking noises were returning again.

"Bitch, why do you always come talking shit when I'm busy? Can't you see I'm driving?" I said to Nicole.

"Stop running Nikki! Pull over!" Nicole replied.

"Your muther-fucking ass might want to go back to the institution, but I'm not going. Raymond Neil can kiss my ass," I said as I drove faster uphill.

"You are going to get us killed, Nikki! Is that what you want?" Nicole screamed at me.

I looked up at Nicole and replied, "I don't know. Feeling lucky, bitch?"

When I said that to her, I drove faster, trying to see just how fast this piece of shit car would go. I took the twists and turns like a pro. I could hear the sirens as the pig gained on me. Damn, I knew I couldn't outrun that Crown Vic.

"Nikki please stop!" Nicole screamed at me, but I gave her a grin then tuned her out.

While trying to get rid of the pig, I had a flash back about Jeremy and me, when we almost wrecked off the slanting cliff not far from where this deserted uphill road was taking me. After it happened, I was pissed because I had never been that close to death. To know that I could have gone off the cliff side made me even angrier at him. Although I did not stay angry long. *I cut my eyes to the left, over at Jeremy. He gave me that smile that I had always loved, and my anger was completely gone.*

"Jeremy pulled over at that spot," I said to myself as I zoomed by it.

We got out the car, and he came over and grabbed me. He hugged and kissed me as he apologized for scaring me. He held my hand as he showed me that the cliff was not as bad as it looked. I walked closer to the edge, and I could see that he was right. He told me that down below was a shallow valley and that the ground was actually softer and not that far if you really looked at it. However, in a car, you would think the cliff was really bad. He had wrecked at that very spot once before.

Thinking of Jeremy, I continued to remember that day as I drove away from the fucking pig. *Jeremy had told me that he and a buddy of his had survived. I smiled as I thought about how excited his face appeared to me as he spoke with such enthusiasm. "Baby, we bailed out the car before it blew up in flames. That must be what saved us."* The memory I was having of Jeremy was disrupted as the policeman ordered me to pull over through his loud speaker. I looked back at him, flipped him off, and smashed the gas much harder. As I came closer to the spot up ahead, I decided to try it. *What the fuck else do I have to lose?* I thought. Because the way the police was coming behind me, outrunning him would be impossible.

I looked over at Nicole and smiled as she shook her head from side to side. I really didn't give a fuck what she was thinking. I wasn't going back to Raymond Neal for her or anybody else.

"Nicole, they already think we have gone off the deep end, so let us show them," I said.

Before she could reply I started counting backwards.

"5, 4, 3, 2..." when I got to "1", I saw the police car stop as I went over the hill. The car was tossed around like a feather as it went to and fro, while hitting the big rocks sticking out from the cliff's side. My body was jumping up and down, while the car proceeded to go deeper down the side of the small cliff. Amusingly, I felt like I was riding a mad dick as my body went up and down in the driver's seat.

I laughed loudly as my adrenaline rushed with anticipation. I then saw the spot Jeremy had warned me about approaching. I focused and pumped myself up more. I used my left hand to open the door as I took my right foot off the gas. The car was going faster now. I glanced at the ground and saw all kind of rocks and grass sticking out.

"Now or never," I said.

With my left hand still on the door, I slanted my body to the left to get out from under the steering wheel. I finally hugged my legs into me and held them with my right arm as I rolled out the car like a ball. Before I could come to a final stop, the car blew up in flames at the base of the hill, not too far from me. I settled against a small tree. I laid there as long as I could. My body was bloody, bruised and in pain, but nothing felt broken, and I was alive. I lifted my head up as far as I could stand it. The car was burning hotly, while the flames were darkened with black smoke.

"What do you think it's going to be like when you go to hell, Nikki? If you can't take this heat, wait until you get there," Nicole taunted me as I lay on the ground hurting.

"Shut the fuck up. You seem to forget; if I go, you go. We burn together, muther-fucker," I said.

I had been beaten by family, had been misused, broken, hurt by the men I loved and, in the end, came up to nothing but another disappointment. I tried to stand, but I staggered backwards and fell back on the ground. I knew that soon the police and fire department would show up, so I found strength and got up. I rubbed my head with my left hand, touched my pocket and discovered my 9mm was still intact after all that bullshit. I looked around for a path Jeremy had told me about; I placed the gun at the base of my back and walked in that direction. I wasn't for sure if that was the path, but I had to get my black ass out of there. The flames were getting too hot, and before long, Nicole would come along, talking shit again. I was hurting and not in the mood for her bullshit.

I managed to make it through the woods, and when I did, my feet came to a desolate highway. The first car drove right past me, so I must've looked horrible. The next few cars zoomed by even faster as I walked slower. When the next car came by, I placed my thumb in the air. However, it went on by too. Hours passed, and the next car finally stopped. I bent down and looked into his face. To me, he looked like a pervert.

I knew the type and had seen them many times before, but right now, he would have to do.

“Where you going, sugar?” the man asked me as he looked me over with a steely gaze.

“I know I look a mess right now, but if you put your car in park and follow me, you will enjoy where I take you. What you think about that?” I replied.

Not giving him much time to respond, I stepped back from the car and walked further off the road. The man pulled over and drove a few feet behind me. Once we were out of sight, I took off my shirt.

As I walked closer to him, he said, “Here.”

He threw me a wet towel. The water felt good upon my skin, but the soap burned a little. Nevertheless, I was feeling clean, albeit topless. I looked back at him, and he had taken his shirt off. I got within arm’s length of him and asked, “You like little girls or little boys?”

“At this moment, I like you bitch,” he replied.

I placed my hands behind me to take off my pants, slowly pulled out my 9mm and pointed it at him. He jumped backwards surprised, and I shot that perverted bitch five times. I reloaded the 9mm and shot him three more times in the face. Pussy-ass muther-fucker.

I went over to him and whispered, “You look dirty, you faceless dirty bastard.”

I spit on the dead, perverted muther-fucker, went through his wallet, got out his cash and walked back to the car. I picked up his shirt and put it on. I closed the car door, cranked up and assed out, driving down the highway.

After I turned off his whack-ass music, Nicole emerged. She looked so damn pitiful, with her sad-ass face. I shook my head and continued to drive. I thought, *This bitch is really going to make me kill her off. Why do I even fucking bother with her?*

I drove for about three more miles. Then, I stopped at the back of the nearest store because I kept hearing a thumping sound coming from within the trunk. I took the keys out of the ignition, looked around and decided to open the trunk. Laying in a fetal position in the trunk was a blond haired young woman. She had a handkerchief on her eyes and a rag in her mouth. Her hands were tied behind her back, and her feet were roped together. Her clothes were torn and bloody, and her appearance was dirty.

This is new. I knew he was a pervert, I thought to myself. I closed the trunk back, moved the car to a more secluded area away from the store, then reopened the trunk. *Click, click, click*. The bitch in my head started talking to me once again, “Let her go. She has nothing to do with this.”

“Bitch will you please, for the life of me, shut the fuck up? I know what the fuck I am doing. Let me run this shit. That is why we are in the shape we’re in. You don’t know how to run nothing. So, please back the fuck up, and let me do this,” I replied.

Nicole said nothing more to me, and for that, I was glad. I began poking the woman with the butt of my 9mm to see if she was dead. When she jumped from the last hit of the 9mm, she caused me to jump backwards. She started crying as the clicking noises invaded my head. *Click, click, click*.

"You again. Why do you keeping fucking with me?" I said with displeasure.

"She is alive. Let her go, Nikki. It is Jeremy you want, not her. She looks like she's been through enough," Nicole said, trying to plead this girl's case.

"If I let her go, will you leave me the fuck alone, so I can think?" I asked.

"Yes! Yes! I will leave you alone for now, so you can think," Nicole replied.

I looked back at the woman, took the rag out of her mouth and said, "If I untie your feet and help you out, will you be a good girl?"

"Oh please! Please! I will not say a word," she pleaded.

I reached inside the car, untied her feet, and helped her out. I pulled the handkerchief off her eyes and stared deep into her blue eyes. She looked back shyly as her eyes adjusted to the light. The young woman stared at me when her eyes adjusted to the light. I then spoke to her in a meaningful tone, "I pulled the handkerchief off your eyes, so you can see who the fuck saved you."

"Thank you so much for saving me," she replied with tears running down her face.

"It is not me that saved you, but a voice in my head. I am going to tell you this only once. You have never seen me, and if you tell someone you saw me, I will find you and kill you," I said.

She stood there, unsure what to do with or think of her newfound freedom. I walked off, then turned back to her. I took my 9mm from my back, touched my temple and said, "Oh yeah! Now, run!"

She looked puzzled at me, then replied, "Run?"

I walked back up to where she stood and pushed her in the other direction. She budged a little. Then, I aimed my 9mm at her. She took off like a rocket. As I watched her run away, I thought about how much I'd played hide 'n' go seek at the park when things were innocent for me. I went back to the trunk and saw a bag. I opened it up and discovered that, yes, it contained more clothes that looked like they would fit me. I picked up a straw hat and placed it on my head. I put on the clothes and closed the trunk. Then, I got back into the car and smiled as I drove off.

Chapter 10

A few hours later, I saw an older lady wearing a nasty-ass dress, hitchhiking. I looked up in the rearview mirror and the clicking began. *Click, click, click*. I drove faster in hopes the clicking would stop. I drove further past the hitchhiker, then Nicole said, "Pick her up. She needs a ride."

"People in hell need ice water, but do you see me giving them some?" I shot back.

"Come on Nikki! What harm could an old lady pushing a shopping cart on a highway do?"

I turned the car around and went back to her. I rolled down the window and asked, "Where you going?"

"I don't know. I just need to get out the sun for now. Will you give me a lift?" she asked.

"You can ride, but your shit can't," I said to her.

"Can I at least gather one or two of my things? Please?" she asked politely.

"I don't mean to be rude, but you need to hurry the fuck up. I got shit to do," I replied.

The old lady put a big bag on the back seat, got in on the passenger side of the car and placed a blanket over her legs. She immediately annoyed me.

"What's your name?" she asked.

"Nikki," I said as I kept my eyes on the highway.

"My name is Mary Ann, but my friends call me Ann. You can call me Ann, being that we will be friends and all," she said as she looked down the road.

"I will call you Mary because I am not your friend," I replied.

"Sounds like you have been riding too long, and have had a rough day, little lady. Is all well with you, today?" she asked.

"Sounds like you don't know how to mind your fucking business and ride," I snapped at her.

"You are right. I am sorry for prying. I am here if you want to talk about it," she said as she looked out the window at the environment and started talking about random things.

A few hours passed, and she was still talking. I did comment, but continued driving. For Nicole's sake, I was tuning the old lady out, but when I heard her say something about little boys and daddies, I had to ask her to repeat herself.

"Excuse me. What did you say about daddies and little boys?"

"My stepson told me he wished I was dead. He told me that his father, my husband, molested him, and I did not believe him," Mary said to me as I looked over at her.

"You didn't? Why do you think he would lie?" I asked her while seeing Nicole's face in the mirror.

"At the age of five, he had a history of being like the little boy that cried wolf, if you know what I mean," she said as she laughed in a condescending way.

"That did not mean that he was lying. Why would you not believe he was telling the truth about something of that magnitude?" I asked her sternly.

"When I met him, he was still sleeping in the bed with his father naked and even bathing with his father. My husband said my stepson started acting like he could not stand me merely because he assumed that I was trying to take his mother's place in his life, but I wasn't. Can you imagine a five year old boy sleeping and bathing with his grown father and resenting his stepmother for coming into their lives?" she asked me, and I looked at her as she continued speaking.

"Back then, even at that early age, he had a history of being clingy and never wanting to be away from his father. His father told me it was his way of getting attention from him. I allowed it to go on, thinking he needed to express himself. At night, I would have my husband read him a story for almost an hour. My husband would come out the room looking sweaty. Then, he would go to sleep. This continued as he got older, from around the age of eight all the way until he was thirteen. He started sitting in his lap and feeding him things like strawberries, even dabbing his mouth with a napkin if some got on the outside of his lips. They would laugh like people that love each other do."

I interrupted her and said, "Hold on. You did not think it was suspicious that he would come out of his room sweating?

How about the boy sitting on his lap? That did not send off flashing lights?"

"No. He told me he had a gland problem. However, my stepson started acting afraid of his father as he got older. He started acting like he regretted story time with him and avoided him altogether. Why would I suspect something was going on?" she asked me.

I drove faster and started thinking about my own fucked up childhood with my father and how no one believed me when I told them that Vanessa's friends had raped me. The memory became all too new to me as I listened to the bitch to my right talk. *Click, click, click.*

"Nikki, get a hold of yourself. You hear me?" Nicole said, trying to calm me down.

"Are you okay, Nikki?" Mary said.

"I'm fucking fine, old lady. Finish your story," I replied slowly and deeply.

"When he was fifteen, I came home from work early and heard noises coming from the boy's bedroom. When I looked in, my life changed. My husband was standing up, while my stepson was on his knees giving my husband, his father, head. My walking into the room disturbed them because my stepson jerked away and cum spilled all over his face. My mouth fell open, and my stepson got off his knees. The only thing my stepson said was, 'I told you he was molesting me, and now he has to hit it from the back with no Vaseline.' He pulled down his pants, and my husband, without saying a word to me, entered his son expeditiously. I cried as I packed up my bags and left the same day. It is my stepson's fault that my marriage failed," she concluded.

I turned my head toward her so hard that I almost snapped my own damn neck. I said, "What the fuck did you say?"

"I said, it is my stepson's fault that my marriage failed. He should have left my husband alone and found his own lover, but he had to entice my husband, his father, to do something he obviously did not want to do," she replied then turned her head back towards the window.

I pulled over to the side of the road and told Mary, "You can get the fuck out now."

"You're putting me out here, in the middle of nowhere?" she asked.

"No, old lady, you can piss here because I'm not stopping any time soon. So get out and fucking piss," I ordered.

She got out as I pulled out my knife. I looked around for any other vehicles, then squatted down next to her and pretended to piss. Before she could get up, I rushed over, jumped on her back and held her in that squatting position.

"What are you doing Nikki?" Mary screamed. *Click, click, click.*

"Leave her alone, Nikki!" Nicole yelled.

"Shut up Nicole," I screamed as I shook the old lady.

"Let her go Nikki, before you hurt her!" Nicole yelled out.

"I will let this unbelieving bitch up when I am ready for her to get up!" I screamed back at Nicole.

"Get off me, you crazy bitch!" Mary screamed.

"Shut the fuck up! Too many of you trying to fuck with my head!" I screamed.

"Get off me Nikki," the lady said again.

"Fuck you bitch! I have to make a believer out of you, for your stepson's sake," I replied, almost out of breath from holding her down.

"I believe him. I believe him. I really do. Just let me go," Mary begged.

"You fucking bitch, you should have protected him," I retorted.

"Get off me!" Mary yelled as a small trail of tears started down her crusty face.

"You should have helped him when you had the chance, but now, no more chances. He said he wished you were dead. Tell your stepson wishes do come true," I said as I lifted the knife and stabbed her with venomous rage. The entire time I was on her cutting her to pieces, she screamed and shook underneath me, but no one could hear Mary cry and beg for her life.

When Mary stopped moving, I paused. I wondered if this bitch was playing dead. Fuck it! I would see if she was really dead or not. I turned Mary over on her stomach; she still did not move. I lifted her dress and cut off her panties. I began slicing the top of her pussy, hoping she would move, but she didn't. If she had moved, I was going to tear her mutherfucking heart out.

I stood up quickly; I thought I heard a car coming. I moved to the back of the car and cupped my ears to make sure. After standing there for a few minutes looking both ways down the highway, I looked over at Mary. I looked out towards the woods, and I saw a big ass stick. I looked at Mary and raised an eyebrow. I heard *Click, click, click* in my head; Nicole's weak ass had something to say.

"Leave that old lady alone," Nicole said.

"Fuck you. I'm about to give this old lady a good fucking," I laughed to myself as I ran toward the woods to pick up the piece of wood.

"Nikki, what's gotten into you?" Nicole asked softly.

"Fuck you Nicole. Stop talking to me muther-fucker," I replied as I picked up the piece of wood and ran back to Mary. I kicked her upside the head to make sure the bitch wasn't breathing.

I squatted down between Mary's legs, took her left leg and bent it backwards. I tried to stuff the piece of wood in her pussy, but it was too small. I picked up my knife and began to dig in her pussy to widen it up. I threw the knife down and stuck the wood in her pussy with no problem. Moving it in and out kind of excited me. I said out loud, "This is for your stepson, you sorry ass excuse for a parent."

After I finished playing around, I stabbed her over and over again. I used the sharp knife to mark her ass and spine because she deserved it for not believing her innocent stepson. The more I thought about her denying it, the deeper and harsher the cutting became.

When I got up, I saw that I'd deeply gutted her with the knife from her asshole to her brain stem. I'd severed the spinal cord and revealed tissue underneath. Blood was everywhere, and pieces of her bones stuck out of her. Pleased with the sight before me, I laughed at the way her back was filleted open.

I looked around and let out a hearty laugh that made me tremble with joy. I turned my head back towards Mary, went over to her and placed her back into the car carefully; she was in a deep sleep now. Next, I neatly placed her dirty looking blanket on top of her legs the way she'd had it and got my straw hat. I carefully put it on her head and pulled the straw hat down over her face, so when the sun came up it would not bother her. I closed the door gently. Then, I went into the trunk, cleaned the blood off me and got out another shirt. I threw down the one I had on, closed the trunk back and smiled at the way Mary was tilted as she rested. I walked to the driver's side and said to Nicole, "Bitch, you always get me in some more shit. Look at what the fuck you made me do to Mary."

"I told you to let her go Nikki, but you are stubborn," Nicole replied.

"I may be stubborn, but I am the one that is not letting anything get between you and Jeremy, you dumb bitch."

"Bye Nikki," Nicole said in an ugly manner, and I did not hear her voice anymore as I got in the car.

I looked over at Mary and said to her, "I guess it is just me and you kid, on the open road and having girl time."

I put the car in gear and drove off. For a day or two, I talked to Mary. She was quiet and really listened to everything I had to say. She did not fuss, whine or complain about anything I did or did not do, unlike Nicole.

More days passed. I got lost but thankfully I asked Mary, and she would just nod. Another day passed, and Mary began to annoy me. Flies were all in the car. I even let the window down, but nothing worked. I finally had to tell her to leave because I refused to endure more of this mess she was causing in the car. I looked over to her and said, "Bitch, you stank worse than you did when you got in here." She did not mumble, because she was always quiet with me. I had to hurt her feelings because she was hurting my nose; therefore, I continued to tell her, "Mary it has been fun, but you got to get your stanking ass out this car. Bitch, you cutting the fuck up in this muther-fucker. Take those damn flies with you. You brought those muther-fuckers with you; you take those muther-fuckers back with you."

I pulled over, got out, and opened the passenger side door to let her stanking ass out. When she was out, she left a scent. I kept the windows down and turned on the defroster, but it smelled like fried ass.

"What the fuck, Mary? You can't possibly still be in this bitch," I said as I got back on the highway in a hurry for some fresher air.

After driving for hours, the sun was down again, and it was nice to have just Nicole and me on the highway, undetected by anyone. Therefore, my mind went to my love Jeremy again and how happy he had always made me. The smell of Mary no longer plagued me, so I continued reminiscing about Jeremy as I drove on the straight highway. *Jeremy is holding me and kissing me tenderly. Everything he says makes me laugh. Oh, how he loves me.*

I could still hear him say, "You are my best friend, and it means so much to me that we are together like this."

"You really mean that Jeremy? You are happy that we are together?" I asked him with happiness all on my face.

"Yes I do. Nicole, I love you and only you. You mean a lot to me," he said as he looked deep into my soul.

"Jeremy, you mean so much to me, and if we marry, it will bring me so much joy to know that I am with you and no one else."

"Nicole, let me make love to you and show you how good I can make you feel," Jeremy said as he looked at me with love in his eyes.

"Jeremy, only you can make love to me, only you," I said as I looked into his handsome face and warm smile.

"Nicole, you are for me, and I am for you. Let me love you like a real man should," he said as he leaned closer to me.

His huge hands cupped my apple bottom ass as I allowed his tongue to play in my mouth. Bedazzled by the kiss Jeremy was giving me, I thought I felt the bright light of the heavens shine on us, but it was really the sight of bright headlights and the sound of a big truck blowing its horn. It snapped me back into reality as I swerved out of the way. After barely missing the head-on collision, I placed my hand on my chest to cover my fast beating heart. I took a few short breaths, and I gathered my thoughts.

"I am so in love with Jeremy, and my love is pulling us closer and closer," I said as I pulled back onto the highway and started back on my journey. Everything was silent until I heard *click, click, click* and the all too familiar voice squeaking in my ears; "Nikki, you are my soul mate, and I miss the fact that we don't talk anymore. I used to be your best friend."

Nicole paused and continued on, “Do you remember how we used to play in our room at night when everyone was asleep? Do you remember how we were never alone and how we always had each other?”

I looked at her pitiful, sad face and replied, “Nicole, I miss you too. You are my best friend. I don’t think I am really yours though. You would only talk to me whenever you were sad or needed to build up your confidence about something. I think you only used me, but now you can’t do that. I am out of your head,” I told her with an attitude.

“Why do you say that, Nikki? When you look in the mirror, don’t you see me? We look just alike, Nikki.” Nicole said with surprise in her tone. I placed my eyes back on the road.

“Not for long, Nicole. After my next stop, I will look totally different, and I will only see you when I look in the mirror,” I said to her in a smart aleck way.

“We were talking about Jeremy and soul mates remember? Not our looks,” Nicole said to change the subject.

“Fine, you said soul mate, Nicole. What about Jeremy? Is he not your soul mate?” I said.

“Not like that, Nikki. Being a soul mate with a man is different. There is no other man for me but him. However, what you and I have is our bond, and no one can break that. As much as I love Jeremy, he can’t even break it,” Nicole said to me.

Seeing the smile on her damn face irritated the cuts and bruises I had received from going over the cliff, so I poured salt in her wounds and said, “How is he your soul mate? Didn’t Jeremy say that he didn’t want you anymore? Didn’t he say he changed his mind about marrying you? Didn't he just want to stay friends with you?"

"Nikki, don't do this. We are making progress," Nicole said.

"No, you dumb bitch! You tell me of the innocent things. What about how he used to talk to you about his bitches? Didn't you love him then as much as you do now? What about the days you cried when he left? Oh, I remember one. How about the time you walked in on him fucking the shit out of the girl next door you invited over for dinner that night?" I began laughing at the dumb bitch.

"Please Nikki, don't dwell on the past. Leave that alone and be happy with me, like you used to be," Nicole pleaded.

"Happy? Why should I let you get all the enjoyment, you weak bitch. I feel happy when I give pain, not while reminiscing about some fucker that hurt me. How in the hell is that happy?" I shot back.

"Nikki, all I am saying is it does not hurt to think about happy times someone has given me," Nicole apologetically said to me.

Realizing what was happening, I laughed an evil laugh. I spoke more fiercely to Nicole than I ever had before. "Bitch, you almost had me fooled and convinced. I was almost like putty in your hands. I was stupid for even giving you a second, third and fourth thought."

Focusing my eyes in the mirror, I told that bitch, "You will never get me weak again with happy thoughts of a shallow man that did nothing but use you. You and your so-called happy thoughts created a monster on a rampage."

I turned the mirror upwards and drove faster down the highway. As I sped with my thoughts out of control, I realized I had to plot the perfect crime. Jeremy had hurt Nicole, and he had caused me to do things that I normally would not do. Just for putting me through shit, he would have to pay. *How do you make a smooth talking muther-fucker like Jeremy pay for making Nicole love him the way she does?* I wondered.

As I drove down the highway, my thoughts became as alive as ever within me. *I could mix lye and water, and then put it down his throat*. I smiled at that, then decided against it. *I know he won't let me get that close to him*. So, I thought on. *I could chop him up and feed him to the alligators in the bayou swamp. No, that wouldn't work, because I don't intend to go through the deep part of the Louisiana area*, I thought on as the highway flashed by.

"Don't worry Nikki. You will think of something," I told myself as Nicole was silenced by my thoughts of revenge. Just another day or two, and Jeremy would be begging me not to take his life. I laughed at the thought. And if Nicole interfered, she would be begging for her life, too. Fuck her.

Chapter 11

Gathering my thoughts, I had to find Jeremy's mother ex-husband. She remarried and divorced after Jeremy's father died. Finally, I came across a very small town where I thought Jeremy's step-father lived, and I told Nicole I needed some items fast as I drove a little further down the highway. At first, nothing was in sight. Then, I drove a few more yards, and to my right, there stood a Co-op store. It appeared to be busy, but I went in anyway.

"Hello. Can I help you, miss?" a young man asked nicely as he walked up to me with a Colgate smile.

"I am just browsing around. If I need some help, I will ask you for sure, little man," I said with a warm smile that was Nicole all over.

I went down every aisle, and I finally found some rope. After looking around, I placed the bundle down my pants. Then, I waved my hand for the naïve little boy to come over, and he did, almost running as he came.

"Do you all sell acid?" I asked.

"Not in large amounts. To be honest with you, miss, we only carry acid out of the battery," he said as we walked.

"So, how do I get it?" I asked nicely.

He turned, and I followed him. The geeky bastard pulled me in the restroom and said, "Let me see and touch your nice sized breasts."

"A gamer after my own heart. Sure," I said as I opened the blouse, and he squeezed my breasts.

"You finished now?" I asked impatiently.

"Yes. As beautiful as those things are, you can have a lot of acid," he replied.

We walked out of the restroom and went outside. Although I only needed one or two, he poured me up a lot of acid in a few bottles. I opened the top and looked at him watching me. I started to give him a dose in his eyes, but someone came over with a question about fertilizer.

"Excuse me," I said as I leaned over to the unsuspecting little boy. "The next time a woman asks you for something, just to give her what she asks for. If you don't, I will make sure your eyes burn and your hands are glued to your young balls for all to see. Consider yourself lucky. Do I make myself clear, boy?" I asked.

He nodded his head quickly as the customer observed us. I walked away, with him looking after me. I left unnoticed with the items and drove off further down the street. I glanced in the mirror and decided that I needed a new look, because this old one was not going to do anymore. Nicole needed to fade away like I told her she needed to. I couldn't be me looking like a bitch like that.

I stopped at a Walgreen's drug store and stole red hair dye and a pair of scissors. *It's easy to steal in this hick ass town*, I thought as I hid the items out of view of the clerk. He was too preoccupied with watching the young black boy who'd come in the store with a white muscle tee and sagging pants that revealed his underwear. I looked away from him, picked up a small plastic case of razor blades and placed them in my mouth. I then walked to the counter and bought a pack of gum. I smiled at the clerk and stole some Upper's right in front of his face.

Now I need somewhere to go to change up, I thought, as my eyes scanned the area as I drove down the highway. About ten minutes later, I pulled into a BP gas station. I paid for some gas and went to the restroom. It was locked so I had to go back in, be nice and ask for a key.

"Excuse me. Could you ever so kindly sir, give me the key to use your ladies' room out back?"

He gave me a creepy smile and said, "Yes, ma'am. You sure can. Around here, we keep the door locked because people steal the tissue. If there is not any in there, come back in, and I will get some for you quickly."

"Could I have a brown paper bag, also? Thank you, sir. I appreciate your kindness," I said.

I took the key and bag from him and walked off, making my firm, little ass shake. Once inside, I checked the water and locked the door. Then, I pulled off my shirt and placed a few pieces of paper towel around my neck before dying my hair. After I finished, the new me made me smile once more as I imagined hairstyles in my head. I decided on a small bang with hair trimmed towards the chin style, so I picked up the scissors and watched my fingers work on my head for the Nikki look and not the weak-ass Nicole look. As the hair fell away from my head and into the sink, another smile came upon my face because I liked the look of a strong and determined Nikki. I ran my fingers through my wet hair and tore the brown paper bags into strips. I used the strips to make curls in my hair, and as soon as I finished, I heard *click, click, click.*

This bitch Nicole was in my head, and I knew she had something to say. I began hitting my head against the wall, but that did not stop her from bumping her gums as she said, "What do you plan on doing with this new look, Nikki? Huh? Tell me? You are destroying my beautiful hair with color."

"What the fuck do you think I plan to do with a different look, bitch? Your look had to go away like you had to go away," I said in anger to Nicole.

"Since it is my body, I have the right to know, don't I?" Nicole said in a questionable tone.

"You had a right to put that damn dog on a leash, but you didn't. Now you don't have any more rights. You gave them to me when I showed up on the scene. Don't you remember saying, 'Nikki help me! I can't do this alone. Please help me stand up and be encouraged.'?"

"Nikki, I didn't mean for all this to happen. You have gone overboard, and I feel like you are trying to make me disappear," Nicole said to me.

"Nicole, that old me was you. She was a weak muther-fucker in dire need of help, and shit, this new look is me. It says I don't play, and if I do, I better win. As for the new look, you like?" I asked as I turned around in circles, admiring the new me.

She was amazed at the results and said, "I don't see me anywhere; I only see you, Nikki. I only see you," Nicole said dryly.

"Bitch, that is the point, I don't need you to downplay a bitch like me with guilt and feelings. Look at what that shit has gotten you— up a stream without a paddle. You were fighting a lost cause until I came and kept it real for you," I said as I shifted my blouse and adjusted my hair more.

"Nikki, I do like the new look, but the old look is the best. It is who we really are."

"Who says it is the best look for me? Surely not you, stupid bitch. You let a piece of lean muscle called a dick make me come alive. You kept all your feelings in. Therefore, I had to wake up and take charge. Why don't you do the shit your conscious ass dreamed of doing? I am doing what you call keeping it real. Besides bitch, I am the real you, the one you dream of being. Now, shut the fuck up," I said to her as I fixed my clothes.

"Maybe you are, but I have a bad feeling that you are turning me into someone I will regret in the future Nikki," Nicole replied.

When I heard Nicole say that I was turning her out to be someone she would regret in the future, I stared at my best friend. My thoughts went bazaar with rage. Therefore, I put my face closer to the mirror and swiftly moved my face back and pretended to throw punches at the mirror. I wanted to hit the mirror to shut this muther-fucker up, but the new me was just now getting over being bruised, so I backed off and redirected my fury.

"Are you trying to get rid of me for good, or what?" Nicole asked politely.

"You stupid bitch, it is because of you being weak that I am on the outside. If you were strong like you were supposed to be, I would still be a figment of your imagination, so why would I get fucking rid of you?"

"True. I only needed you for a short while, but you are coming in and rearranging everything. You kill, lie, and steal. Now, you are changing our look, so one can't help but watch, wonder and assume that you are up to something without me," Nicole said to me.

I gave Nicole one last hateful look, then waited for about thirty minutes and took the brown paper bag out of my hair. I had learned to do that trick years ago when my mother used to put curls in her hair with a brown paper bag. Vanessa and I had learned from her. Removing the bag strips revealed beautiful curls. I shook my head again to make the curls look lively since they were still a little damp. I then left the restroom and took the key back inside the store.

"Here is your key," I said to the man as I held out my hand.

"Damn young lady! You look good. I had forgotten all about that key," he replied.

"Yes you did. I see you didn't come looking for it," I said.

"A lot of times, customers leave the key in the bathroom and we have to go get it or wait until another costumer comes in, and we have to give up the spare key, hoping that they will bring it back," he explained.

"Oh okay. I do apologize for keeping it so long," I replied.

"It's no problem, Ms. Lady. You do look good," he said, waving as I exited the store.

Before I could reach the car, I heard, "Lady, you look good. Want some company?" from a man as I walked towards my car.

I stopped and observed who the fuck it was that was halting me from getting in my car. When I saw just how not ready he was for the shit I could bring, I said, "Fellow, you don't want this shit. I promise you don't."

"How about letting me be the judge of that?" he replied.

As I recalled how Mary Ann had fucked up my car with her smell, I decided there was no way in hell I was going to lay in that bitch and do shit. I replied. "Go in the men's restroom, and when no one is looking, I will come in. Have your pants already off because I am in a hurry," I said.

He went into the restroom. I took a razor out of the small plastic container in my mouth and followed him. The bathroom door swung back towards me after I walked in, and I began fondling him as he sat on the toilet. Before he knew what had happened, I swiped his dick swiftly with the blade. I kept squeezing and sliced two more times, leaving his dick in two pieces. He was licking his lips and bouncing himself on the toilet to tease me. He was no longer rock hard while he sat on the toilet. *What a pathetic sight*, I thought with such distaste. He did not feel a thing. This man had no idea that his dick now laid split open like a hot dog bun that had been sliced open three times instead of once. He continued to bounce as the

blood dripped into the toilet. I tried to contain my laughter but could not.

"Why are you looking at me and laughing? Get in here," he said.

"I can't because you are bleeding, and I think you are going to need a doctor," I said as I glanced down and eyed his pants.

"I don't need a doctor; I'm good and hard," he said.

I pointed my left index finger to his once solid pecker, and he looked down. The man opened his mouth to scream, but before he could, I sliced his muther-fucking mouth from cheek to cheek. He fell to the floor, and I sliced him a few more times across the mouth and face. He lay on the floor with his eyes bucked and mouth hanging open. I started to fuck him up some more, but had to get the hell out of there before they found his body. I was becoming unglued. I had to get the fuck away from there. Before I left, I stared at the man as he laid on the floor.

"Search him to see if he has any money in his pockets. Look for some keys because Mary's smell is still in the car," I spoke to myself. I searched his pockets and found a few dollars and some car keys. I snatched them up, cleaned up and left. Damn, I was bound to get caught fucking off with these fools. They were stopping me from getting to my destination.

I eased out towards the car, then looked on the ring to see which vehicle it was. After I found the car, I drove it near the other car I had and placed my weapons in his car. I drove the old vehicle I had to the back of the store and parked it, hoping nobody would see me or ask any questions.

Nicole said, "Nikki, you never cease to amaze me."

"Damn bitch! I never cease to amaze myself," I laughed.

I cranked up his car and continued to laugh as I left.

After driving nine blocks over, I arrived on Yellow Wood Street. All the houses on the street looked just alike and finding the right one appeared to be hard to do. I drove slower and cruised around looking for the house Jeremy had taken me to. Twelve houses later, and there it was. I saw the house I had been searching for. The house was a bright orange with deep black shutters. The overhead hangers were white, and the windows had black out screens. Everything seemed normal, so I decided to park the car on the opposite side of the street to check any activities that might be coming from the house.

All of a sudden, a tall thin man appeared. He seemed to be around the age of fifty or more. He came out of the house wearing pajamas and slippers and picked up the morning newspaper. I thought he saw me because he seemed to look right at me, but I guess he didn't, because the older man dropped his head and went back in.

I reached under the seat and picked up a twenty ounce bottle of battery acid, two feet of short rope, and two four feet rope strips. I also grabbed a retractor, a few razor blades and my 9mm. I placed them all in a small bag that I found in the vehicle, and after clamping the bag shut, I took one last look at the new me and got out the car. I looked around and did not see anyone coming. So, I adjusted my skirt and opened my blouse to expose my breasts and thighs. Shaking the homemade curls in my hair, I walked up to the front door. I knocked on the door, and waited for his "former step-father" to open up. When he did, I gave him a joyous smile as his eyes explored my breasts and my face. He asked, "May I help you?"

"Yes! May I come in, sir?" I answered.

"Yes, come on in," he said with a smile, but without asking why.

As he closed the door, I moved to the side and noticed the back door. "Perfect," I said to myself.

"I am looking for a Jeremy Bland. Does he live here?" I asked.

"Sit down, you pretty thing," he said as he sat down. I sat before him and crossed my legs to make sure my thighs were showing.

"Who are you? I have never seen you before, but something about you seems so familiar to me. Are you sure we have never met?" his father asked me as he stared at my features closely.

"I am a news reporter. You might have seen me on TV or somewhere reporting news about ordinary people that have done well for themselves," I said as I touched my breast area to remove his eyes from my face.

"No," he said as he watched my hand play with the buttons on the blouse. "I don't think it was that. Are you sure we have never met? Someone as lovely as yourself would leave an impression on whoever is in your presence."

He continued to stare, and what he had said was true. When I had met him for the first time with Jeremy, he told me I was lovely and remarked that his son had picked a winner with me. That was short lived because his son Jeremy called it off, and we just remained friends. I smiled back at his father and replied, "I want to do an interview on Jeremy and how his life is going now."

"Well, Jeremy is not around; he is not here. I don't know where he is. This time of year, there's no telling where that son of mine is off to," he said nicely.

"Can you give me his number, address or anything?" I asked.

"I don't feel that I should just give out that information, especially since I don't know you and all," he said as he stood up.

"Sir, you don't know me, but you invited me into your home," I pointed out.

"Yes, I did, and now, I am ending this conversation, but you can leave your name and number here with me. That way, when I talk to him, I can get him to give you a call back," he replied.

He handed me a piece of paper, so I wrote down Misty Parkston 661-662-3566. I handed him the phony information and left. As I went back to the car, I saw him watching, so I got in the car. I drove around the block and returned quickly. I parked two houses down and got out my hand shovel. I went to the back of the house, eased in the back door and heard him saying, "Jeremy, this is your father. Call me ASAP. There's something fishy going on here."

I raised my shovel and cut the conversation short by knocking him the fuck out. I hung up the phone and hit him a few more times to knock him unconscious. Blood oozed all over his salt and pepper hair as it came out the back of his skull. I smiled at the back of him. "Bet you wished you would have told me what I wanted before all this happened, huh?" I said.

I went outside, brought a lawn chair inside, and, after looking around, placed it in the middle of the living room. I struggled to pick him up bit by bit until I had him in the ¾ sitting position. I took the strips of four feet rope and tied one around his chest and chair. Then, I took the other one and tied it around his legs and the chair. I also tied his hands and feet with the other rope for extra coverage, in case he tried to get up. I turned his face toward mine.

"Jeremy looks so much like you. It's hard to believe that you are not really his father. I wonder if I would've fallen madly in love with a son of yours, if he looked just like you," I said as I kissed him softly on the lips.

As he started to wake up, I took the retractor and opened his mouth. His eyes popped open, and he stared at me with his gray eyes. I decided to wait before I talked to my ex-father-in-law. I went into his kitchen to see what food he had.

"Pops, I am damn hungry. I hope you have a lot of food in here," I said as I ate a slice of peach pie. I looked at his father looking at me as I continued, "If you have ice cream, I'll let you go." I looked in the freezer, and there was no ice cream.

I glanced back at him and said, "No ice cream. Guess I have to eat alone." *Click, click, click* went my fucking head as it began banging.

"You act like you don't know how to eat alone," Nicole said to me as I ate the pie slowly.

"In case you have not learned anything, fly bitches don't eat alone. Isn't that right, Pops?" I said as I looked over at Jeremy's father.

After I finished eating my pie, I walked over to Jeremy's once upon a time father. I looked down at him, and my mind began to wonder if his dick was bigger than Jeremy's. I unbuttoned his pants as he squirmed, not wanting me to touch him. After I struggled to get his pants and boxers down, his dick lay exposed. He was bigger and longer than Jeremy. As I stood playing with his dick, it began to rise. I smiled because I thought I would have had to make him get it up. I bent down at his dick and began blowing my hot breath over him. As I touched and blew on him, he became hard as a rock. I placed my mouth on his hard dick. I sucked and sucked him until he was good and ready.

"Are you really going to fuck him?" Nicole questioned.

"Not now Nicole," I spoke.

"Don't fuck him, please. I beg you," she pleaded.

"Leave me the fuck alone," I snapped because his dick was getting soft.

Nicole did as I demanded. I started back sucking him harder and harder, making that dick stand up like it was going to war. I looked up and saw his eyes roll to the back of his head. I sucked his dick like a wild woman. I wanted to fuck. I began pulling down my pants as I continued to suck him. After my pants were off, I mounted him. I grabbed the tip of his dick and guided him into my pussy. I moved inch by inch until I got it all in. He moaned, and so did I. I rode him like a raging bull, bucking to get a cowboy off his back. As I thrust on him, he tried to move with me. We stroked and stroked until his body began to jerk. I got off him and started sucking his dick as nut rushed in my mouth. It was hot. I held the nut in my mouth, stood over him and spit it in his face. His nut fell into his eyes as I laughed. He began jerking his head from side to side trying to get the nut off his face. I laughed at the sight. I should have spit it in his muther-fucking mouth.

I walked back into the kitchen. I started to eat another piece of pie. I offered, "Do you want a piece of pie?"

He closed his eyes. I took the knife out of the bag I had brought in earlier; I got up and rushed over to him, and stabbed him smack in the top of the middle of his head. Blood oozed out the big cut ,and I started slapping on him with the knife. I didn't need him out of it until I got what I needed to know from him. He opened his eye groggily. I took out the twenty ounce bottle of acid, straddled him and said, "Now muther-fucker, tell me what the fuck I want to know. Where the hell is Jeremy?"

His eyes bucked, and he shook his head. His words were barely audible as he mumbled the word, "No."

"No? Nobody tells me no. You have lost your muther-fucking mind, but I guess I will have to give you a wakeup call," I snapped.

I opened the bottle and dropped a few drops of acid into his mouth. He bucked like a child in hot water. I put the top back on it and waited for a few minutes before I started back talking to him.

"You ready to tell me what I want to know?" I asked.

Realizing he could not speak properly, I loosened the retractor and he mumbled, "1740 Maple View Drive in Wells, Nevada."

I wrote the address down, and I got off him. I began pacing the floor again. *Click, click, click*. I dropped the bottle, and began screaming and yelling for the pain in my head to stop, but Nicole was coming with more power. I took both of my hands, grabbed my head as the clicking sound became louder and yelled, "NO! NO! NO! Not you again bitch! Leave me alone! Leave me alone! I'm working!"

"Nikki, you have the information you need; now, let him go," Nicole said in a strong voice.

"You stupid bitch, if I let him go, he will tell on me. I can't let him go. We can't go back there," I replied.

Smack, smack, smack. Nicole began slapping me harshly. I could not stop her from hitting me at first. Then, I grabbed her right hand with my left and twisted her wrist. Nicole did not know how to handle pain, so I kept on twisting her wrist as she complied, saying, "Fine, Nikki. Let go of my wrist. Let my wrist go, okay? Do what you want. He is not worth the pain of you twisting on me."

"Thank you, bitch. I knew you would twist around my way," I said as I turned back to this fake as Jeremy look alike. I swiftly approached him and got within ear shot of him before I said, "That bitch wants me to let you go, but I just can't let you go. Jeremy looks like you so much it pains me to let you live. You must die."

I walked closer to him with tears streaming down my face. I screamed at him as I said, "You have to die, old man, all because your son broke Nicole's heart! You have to pay the price until I see him again!"

I paced back and forth, trying to get rid of my tears because I was not focused. Every time Nicole got power, she appeared quicker, and I couldn't think straight. I sniffled and shook, then dried my face and nose on my shirt. I straddled his big dick again. This time, I opened the top of the bottle and threw it off. I looked down at him and said, "This is going to hurt you more than it hurts me."

My ears were not fully prepared for the sound I heard as I started pouring the acid slowly down his throat. I got off him and watched as he bucked and tried to get loose, but it was all in vain because the ropes held him down tightly. However, some acid splattered on me, and I got angry. I jumped back on top of the strapped body, but, this time with a razor, and started slicing his legs and thighs. I told him, "Nicole doesn't like pain, and no one will hurt Nikki ever again."

When I looked at the spot of acid on my skin, I became outraged. The razor cuts to his lower body became more and more gruesome than ever, as I continued to slice him.

"Calm down, Nikki. Jeremy's father cannot hurt you anymore," Nicole said.

"Bitch, I have to make sure he is dead." I began slicing some more of his thighs until this weak muther-fucker began to say, "He's done, Nikki. Trust me. He's done."

I was splattered in blood, and my arms and hands were covered with the dark red coating. I turned my head slightly to the right and saw Nicole in the mirror. She had tears in her eyes, so I walked over to her and placed my hand on the mirror as she placed her hand on mine.

"Nicole, this is for you. Remember that," I said as I moved away from the mirror.

I was finished with him. I could see nothing but bones, tendons and strips of torn flesh. Everywhere the razor had touched, a thin strip of bloody meat was in its place. As I watched the body that I had sliced up be eaten by acid, a feeling of relief came over me. I picked up the remaining portion of the bottle of acid and burned Nikki into his chest. I liked the way my name sunk inside of him, like the way his son's name had sunk inside of me.

Silently, I cheered his death on. I took the dish detergent and washed the blood from my face and hands. I pulled my hair back into a knot and began looking around for anything of use.

"My dad always keeps a wad of cash in the blue canister on the counter," Jeremy said, as I thought about a previous conversation I'd had with him in the kitchen. I looked where Jeremy said and got the money that was always hidden in the kitchen canister. It was exactly where Jeremy told me he kept emergency cash. It was almost a thousand dollars. I liked this shit.

"Killing is so much more fun than being a good girl. Take notes bitch, and learn how to keep muther-fuckers in check." I went into his room, found some of Jeremy's mother's old clothes and changed into them. They were not too hot, but right now, I would work with them.

I went out the side door and went in the garage and saw Jeremy's father's car. I let the sun visor down, and the keys fell into my lap. I cranked the car, saw the tank was full of gas and, after searching, found more extra cash in the hidden compartment of the car console. I closed the driver's door and left for the address his father had given me.

Chapter 12

Wells, Nevada was beautiful. The small town looked peaceful; the wind was blowing lightly as it eased through the car window, and the air was fresh and clean as it entered my nostrils. I took a deep breath, inhaled the air, closed my eyes, and opened them again. I stopped at a gas station, opened the glove compartment, and got out more money for gas. After pumping the gas, I got back in and headed towards the address. I could not find it, so I had to pull over and ask for directions. I put the car in park and stopped the first car I saw.

"Excuse me, sir. I am looking for the home of Jeremy Bland."

"Jeremy Bland?" the man said as he looked over and asked the person on the other side of him. They talked for a few moments before he turned back to me and replied, "Sorry. Can't help you."

Then, he drove off.

I looked around and saw a woman and her two children. I drove over and said,

"Excuse me. Do you know where a Jeremy Bland lives?"

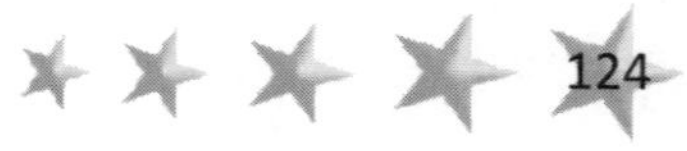

"I don't give out that information, miss," she said as she drove off in a hurry.

"Miss, I hear you are looking for Jeremy Bland. Is he in some kind of trouble?" a man approached me and asked.

"No sir. He is family, and this is my first time out here. You can say I am lost. Can you help me?" I replied.

"Yeah, I know Bland. His place is about fifteen minutes from here," the man answered.

"Sir, could you be more specific?" I asked with a nice warm smile.

"Sure, you see that signal light?"

I looked where he was pointing and said, "Yes."

"Well, take the left at that signal light and go ten minutes on that highway. When you get to a four way stop, take the right, and it should be the first blue house you come across," he said.

"Thank you so much," I replied as I put the car in drive.

Before I could drive off, he asked, "Who did you say you were?"

"I'm a family member who has never been here before. Thank you," I said as I drove off quickly.

Confident I had the right directions, I drove off in a hurry. I drove around for another hour, and I finally found the house. It did not look exactly like the house, but the color was very similar. If this was not the correct address, maybe whoever was inside would help me. I turned the car off, and no one came outside. I saw someone peeping out the window and a funny feeling swept over me. *Click, click, click.*

"Nikki, prepare yourself. This could be it," Nicole said to me in a worried voice.

"Bitch, have I ever let us down? Fuck no, but thanks anyway. I'm a step ahead of you," I replied.

"I was just saying Nikki. Don't be so defensive. I'm on your side," Nicole said.

"Well bitch, I can't tell sometimes. Now shut the fuck up while I go check," I retorted.

I got the sharp butcher's knife and taped it to my left thigh. I grabbed the small container of razors and placed them in my mouth. A man came outside. He looked well-kept but older. He waved a friendly wave for me to get out, and I did.

"Hello! Can you please tell me if Jeremy Bland lives here?" I asked.

He looked at me from head to toe then replied, "You are new here, aren't you?"

"Yes. I am trying to find Jeremy Bland. Does he live here?" I asked getting agitated.

"Hold on. Let me see if he is in," the man said as he walked about five feet up the cobble stone drive way. He opened the door and said something. He came back out and said, "Sure, he's here. Come on in."

I got out, and he came up behind me. Opening the front door was the last thing I remembered.

"Wake up, pretty bitch," I heard a man say. I opened my eyes. I was naked and tied to a small, child sized twin bed, which I did not fit properly on. I turned my head to check out my surroundings. The room was a basement. Pipes were reaching up to the floor, a washer and dryer were in one corner and boxes of items were stacked up all around the room. I turned my head the other way and saw a younger man sitting on the steps. I replayed the voice that had awakened me, and it matched the man watching me. I was not gagged, so I asked him, "Who are you? Why am I tied up?"

He approached me and touched my stomach. His hand reached for my face, so I closed my eyes. He replied, "It does not matter who I am. All you know is that you are tied up."

He took a needle off of a small box and shot the medicine into my veins. I began to black out, but before I passed all the way out, I felt him on top of me pushing his dick in and out of my pussy. I was helpless and could not do anything but let him fuck. I didn't remember when he finished.

When I awakened again some hours later, I was alone and disorientated. I shook my head from side to side and I saw food next to me. I closed my eyes and thought, *Someone is going to pay for this shit*. A door opened, so I turned towards the sound, and the older man was in my vision with the young man behind him.

"Here. You have to eat," he said as he tried to push an oatmeal type food down my throat. I did not eat it, because if I had, I would have killed myself choking on it, and no way was I letting that happen.

"You have to keep your strength up. My boy likes your body," he said as he wet my face with water.

"What do you want with me?" I asked as I gathered my breath.

"Is it not known to you? We are men, and beautiful women like yourself would not give us the time of day," he said as he tied his arm with a small, yellowish plastic hose. He lit up a cigarette puffed it, took another needle and shot himself in the vein. He sat on the stool slumped over, moaning something, before the cigarette fell out of his mouth. *These mutherfuckers are giving me heroin*, I thought as I kept my eyes on the old man. He gave me a creepy smile and came towards me. He picked up another needle and started shooting me up with drugs. I started feeling dizzy. When I looked at him again, he was naked and touching his dick as if to measure it before climbing on top of me. The few moments he was on top of me seemed longer because the old man suppressed me more by choking me as he bounced up and down while fucking me. I was beginning to pass out again when I heard him say right before his orgasm, “I hate women like that.”

I could not breath, and my mind was not functioning as I felt his warm semen roll down my vagina and onto the bed. He lay on top of me a little longer than usual.

The son climbed on top of me next, while his father sat there and watched.

“Let that bitch know who is fucking her,” his father said as his head wobbled left to right. At that point, his son began ramming me with anger, and the pain was worse than any I had ever experienced. I could not beg or plead. My mouth was dry, and words could not form as the young man roughly rode me for hours at a time. His orgasm was much harder to stand, as he made bite marks over and over on my shoulder with his mouth. When he would finish, the father would regain his strength and take off where his son had left off. Although his treatment was painful as well, his was easier to take. That was if I didn't die with his hands around my throat.

Over the next couple of days, I was drugged and raped repeatedly by the father and son. My pussy was sore. My arms were drained from being held up high for a long time, and I was hungry. My stomach growled, and I reached to touch it. That was when I noticed that all the roughness had worked my arms out of captivity. I took my arms out and let them regain their feeling; I loosened the ropes on my feet as well. Over time, I would stand up and stretch, but, when I thought someone was coming, I would place my feet through the loose ropes, place my arms back and hold the ropes with my fingers. If no one showed up, I would take them down again and remove the razors to give my mouth a break. *Tonight, I would replace myself in the position they had me in and wait on whoever came first*, I thought as I placed a razor in my hand.

"Nicole, we will be leaving soon, so hold on." She didn't answer me, so I got angry and laid back down. The time was coming for one or both of them to come in to rape me.

Another day or two must have passed, when the son awakened me as he came in to wash my body off, I pretended to be still out of it as I jumped at his touch.

"Pretty lady, calm down. I don't bite. Well yes I do! Especially when the pussy is just so good and I have to hold my nut back for a little bit longer," he laughed as he wiped me softly while washing me off.

"You're the best piece of ass I have ever had. I think you should know that," he said as he wiped my thumping pussy area.

"Why won't you let me go?" I asked.

He looked up from my pussy and slapped me a few times across the face.

"Why let my pussy go?" he slapped me again and harder.

This time, when he slapped me, Nicole said, "Nikki, do your thing. Get us out of here. I can't take this pain anymore."

Nicole allowed tears to flow from her face. He stopped slapping me and began wiping my tears away with his hand. In a much kinder tone, he said, "I'm sorry. When I heard you talking about leaving me, I panicked. I can't just let you go, you know. It's like, I'm finally able to make love to a woman and not to my hand or little boys," he said.

Click, click, click rang out louder in my head.

"Nikki, you hear that? He sleeps with little children," Nicole whispered in my head.

"I need to go to the bathroom," I said deviously as the young man eyed me up and down.

He got up and placed a bed pan under me. Only a little piss came out. He removed the pan and poured it out in a bucket. The young man then re-wiped me to remove any extra piss from me. He took off his clothes and got on his knees at the end of the bed. He massaged my feet, and then, the inexperienced young man sucked my toes one by one. He then licked the bottom of my feet and bit at my ankles. I remembered when Jeremy put my toes in his mouth, but this mouth was sloppy and unlike my love's. He was making a trail up my legs, and I could tell that his trail of kisses was wet; I felt grossed out, but played along with him.

With tears, Nicole said, "Please make him stop. He will never ever be Jeremy. I don't want him touching me anymore." I smiled at Nicole and bowed my head to her.

When the young man entered me, I kissed him under his neck, throwing him off key by responding as he made pretend-love to me. The young man closed his eyes and became so involved and carried away with me arching my body to receive his thrusts that he did not notice how my arms were hanging out the ropes. With the razor in my hand, I said before I sliced his throat, "Muther-fucker, you forgot to drug me."

When he opened his eyes, his blood poured everywhere. He jumped up holding his throat, but it was too late. I was up with him as he lay on the stairs, naked and facing downward. I grabbed his black hair in my hand and sliced his skin underneath it.

"This cut is for all the times you raped me." *Slice, slice* behind the neck.

"This cut is for slapping me in the face." *Slice, slice* around the ears.

"And this cut is for making Nicole cry." With one final swooping slice around his face, the young man's scalp was in my hand. I scalped that bitch like an Indian.

I threw his scalp in the corner behind a box. I checked around me, snatched his body down the lower steps and placed him in the bed, with the little strength I had left. I tied him up, cut his dick off, and placed it in his ass. His asshole was very small, so I took my knife and grinded and grinded until his ass was fully open. Now, he knew how I felt when he fucked me in my ass. I smiled at the thought that now he was fucking himself with his own dick sitting in his ass.

What a candid moment, I thought. I checked his clothes and found the key. *They must lock the door whenever they are down here with me*, I thought. Then, I tiptoed up the stairs and unlocked the door with the key. I slowly went back down the squeaky staircase and cleaned myself up with the water he'd brought in. Before I could dress, I noticed a knife at the end of the bed. I found some clothes to put on and placed the knife on me. I sat down and ate the food he had brought in. It did not look all that good, but I was hungry as hell, and desperate times called for desperate measures.

Hours had passed, and there was still no sign of the father. I was beginning to think I'd miscalculated the time, but I was right, because soon I heard a few footsteps and knew his father would be coming down in a few minutes. I only had a few moments, so I had to be ready. As I paced the floor, I accidentally knocked over a box and in it were hunting weapons and a Samurai sword; the thing that really caught my eye was the automatic cross bow. I picked up the weapon; I began to get happy and the days I'd spent trapped mattered no more. I put the sword on top of the box as I went and sat under the steps; I decided to wait there for the father to come. I cleared everything out the way so when I aimed at him, it would be a clear shot. I stood up and glanced back over the room. I needed to make sure everything was lined up, I couldn't afford any mishaps.

I sat back under the stairs and remembered the times I had seen hunters on TV shoot a regular bow and arrow and an automatic crossbow. They would hold their hands steady, close their eyes, and aim accurately, usually resulting in a perfect hit every time. With that thought, I loaded the weapon. The father came downstairs, as soon as I loaded the arrow in the chamber, leaving me no time to practice. He walked right past me and went over to where I had once laid in the bed. The old man saw his son, turned, and an instant later our eyes locked. Before he could come towards me, I lifted the bow and arrow up towards him.

"Come on, little lady. Put the weapon down before you hurt your pretty little self," he said as he took a step towards me.

"Don't come any closer. If you do, I will shoot you in the head," I said loud enough for him to hear me.

"Why would you want to do that? We treated you nicely," he said as he walked a step closer to me.

"I will not warn your ass again. Don't come any damn closer to me!" I yelled.

"Come on baby. I will not hurt you. I promise," he lied with a devilish look on his face.

"Back up!" I warned.

Click, click, click.

"Not now, Nicole. I'm too busy for your shit," I said.

"Nikki, Jeremy promised me that too, didn't he?" Nicole asked me.

He smiled and said, "Ok."

He walked backwards as he held his hands up in the air. "See, I am listening to you. I am walking away from you. I am even in open view against the wall for you to see. Drop your weapon, so neither one of us gets hurt."

"Sure. Why not drop it?" I said as I released the arrow. It made a thumping sound as it hit him in his chest.

"You bitch! You shot me with a fucking arrow," he said as he ran towards me. I did not allow him to come all the way to me, but ran towards him as well. We locked up and the arrows were dangerously close to my head. The more I struggled, the more he came closer to penetrating those arrows into my head. Suddenly, I raised my knee up and kneed him in the groin area. His grip loosened as I pulled away from him. Standing up straight now, the old man looked at me and said, "I'm going to smash you on top of me, bitch."

As if I had seen it in my head, he came running towards me with the arrow sticking out of him, but with catlike reflexes, I ducked and cut him in half with the sword. His feet kept on going, but his top half fell to the ground, landing on his back. I picked up a cement block, and threw it down on him and jumped on it.

I looked around for my shoes, then found a knapsack full of weapons and bullets. *This must be my lucky-ass day*, I thought as I put on my shoes. I felt like a woman out for blood. I placed a double edged knife in my hand and put the knapsack on my back, vowing to kill anyone that got in my way.

Opening the door was not a problem, but there sitting on the couch was. A child about the age of ten sat watching TV as I peeped out the door. I closed the door and eased back down the stairs to think. *Click, click, click*. I began shaking my head roughly. I fell to my knees as the pain became more and more persistent. I growled loudly as the room began to turn in circles.

"Nicole, you have to stop making those noises in my head," I said as I gathered myself and stood up with my hands on my aching head.

"Don't kill the child, Nikki," Nicole whispered.

"Why the fuck not? That child probably sat on his ass as his folks were going in and out of my ass," I told her.

"Leave the child alone. Just knock him out, but don't kill him." Nicole pleaded.

"Why not kill the fuck out of him? I need to just in case he decides he wants to follow in their footsteps one day," I replied.

I looked through the bag and found poisonous darts and a mouth blower. As I loaded the blower I said, "I want the entire family of fuckers to die." Simmering with rage, I placed a dart in my hand and a dart in the dart blower. Tiptoeing lightly, I went back up the stairs and cracked the door open. I really felt like an original warrior, on the hunt and out of control.

I caught the boy off guard when I blew the first dart. It stuck him in his leg. He looked around, and I tried to reload the dart gun again but dropped it. As the little boy cried, I walked up to him. Before he could get out a louder cry, I sliced his neck with one of the razors. He didn't feel shit, but fell into my arms. I dropped him quickly because I didn't want any blood on my clothes. He lay out and I didn't care as blood oozed from his neck. His relatives didn't care if they hurt me, and I didn't care if I hurt him. This shit was beginning to piss me off. I was behind schedule and behind bad.

I peeped outside the door then tried to walk normally to their F150 truck. The neighbors were all closed up in their homes. I looked around and saw the keys were still in the ignition.

"Yes," I said as I backed out and this time, headed to the right house of Jeremy Bland.

Chapter 13

I finally saw the house the man had described.

"How ironic. I was only a block off. Well, I'll be alright," I said as I parked the truck in the driveway. I took inventory of the sight before me. "This seems like the house that Jeremy and I once dreamed about," I thought as I continued to stare at Jeremy's house. It was a two story, blue Victorian style home with heavy maroon shutters. The front door was even maroon and the welcome mat was black. The yard was freshly cut and the smell of grass was in the air. A white picket fence surrounded the house, and the fence door was on the side where the cars were to be parked.

This looks like the dream house we had once talked about. *This seems so surreal*, I thought, but my gut told me something different. To the left of the front door was a big wheel, a regular swing, a small sand box with toys. There was also a kiddy pool and a tire swing in the tree nearby. I stared harder at the tire swing and was amazed at how much it reminded me of what I wanted to have with Jeremy. I gazed back at the house; I had a feeling that the kitchen was where I saw the bay

windows. I bet that this is the same house Jeremy and I had designed together when we were a couple. I remember we planned for the family room to open up into the kitchen. The bedrooms would be on the top story, while the spiral stairs would be in the corner of the room with the guest bedroom and full bath to the left. Tilting my head to the right as my eyes partially closed, a light popped on in my head.

"If I didn't know better, I would say our dreams have come to life, but without me," I said as I crossed my purse over my shoulder, got out the truck and walked slowly to the front door.

"Nikki, what's going on?" Nicole said as she began to hyperventilate.

"Shut up," I whispered at her.

"I can't think straight, Nicole, with your nagging. Shut up bitch," I continued.

"Find out what is going on," Nicole said softly.

"Bitch, you are really beginning to talk too much. Let me handle this. Now that I have found Jeremy, you want to talk sweetly to me. That shit isn't going to fly," I replied.

"I just want to know if he still loves me. That's all," Nicole whispered.

"He's going to love the tip of my knife once I lay eyes on him. Believe that," I replied.

I did not quite know what to do because I was still in shock from what I was seeing. Ignoring Nicole, I made myself ring the doorbell. No one came, so I rang it again, and I heard a voice say, "One minute please."

"Is that a woman's voice?" I asked as I anticipated the opening of the door.

A plump older woman with gray hair, who appeared to be around sixty something, opened the door and said, "Yes, may I help you?"

Stunned, I forced a reply. "I am looking for a Mr. Jeremy Bland. Does he live here?"

"Yes, he does, and who are you to be asking?" she asked politely.

"I am Nikki, a classmate of his," I smoothly lied.

She opened the door wider and showed me in as she replied, "Child, come on in. Any classmate of his must be a friend to me."

She shut the door and walked in front of me. She then, said loudly, "I'm Rose, by the way."

I walked slowly behind her, and I was astounded at the sight of the house. It looked like my house with Jeremy had come alive. Everything was in the order that I believed it would be, and the room colors of the house were perfected to the fullest. The Queen Anne furniture was beautiful, and it matched the carpet and drapes perfectly. Tears swelled in my eyes and hatred filled me now more than ever. *I know this shit is not happening to me*, I thought as I was led to the living room that I had designed a million times in my sleep. She saw my eyes touring the house and said, "You like the way my daughter and Jeremy did their home?"

"Yes, ma'am. I love it," was all I could say. Her words "my daughter" stunned me.

"Daughter? What daughter?" I asked in a dumbfound way.

"Yes, my daughter. Have a seat, child," she said as she pointed for me to sit down across from her. I sat down, but my thoughts were running wild like a muther-fucker.

"You said 'daughter', ma'am. How does Jeremy know your daughter?" I pressed.

"Child, they are married," she said as she looked into my face.

"Jeremy is m-m-married," I stammered.

"Child, would you like something to drink?" Rose said to me.

"Uh," I said as I stuttered. Then my voice returned, and I said, "No thank you. I'm not thirsty."

Seeming to not notice my distress, she took a sip out of her tea and crossed her legs before she spoke to me again. However, I was still thinking about the words "Jeremy is married", but not to me. I forced myself to be quiet, but was about to speak to her politely as I could, but rage was coming forth in haste. She removed the tea glass from her lips and spoke before I did.

"I saw your eyes being taken by the house. You like the house?" she asked again.

Forcing a reply, I responded, "Yes, it is wonderful. It is quite exquisite. Where did such a design come from?"

She smiled as she said, "Jeremy had the plans before my daughter came along. He said someone gave him the idea, and he loved it. When he met my daughter Donna, they decided to get a home built. He showed her the layout, and she fell in love with it. Actually, she said it was as if the designer of this home plan was designing this for themselves. Jeremy insisted to her that the one that originally designed the home was not planning on doing anything with the design for a long time, if ever. So, unable to resist the beautiful plans any longer, they had the home built about a year ago, I would say."

I thought back to where I was about a year ago. I was in Raymond Neil Institute. I was lonely and confused about everything going on around me. Jeremy was not there and so much had happened. I lowered my head, and a knife entered my heart at the thought of him making our dream home with another woman.

She took another sip of her tea and said, "Look at me going on and on about Jeremy and Donna."

"Do they have children?" I asked as my voice squeaked.

"Well, she has a six year old son named Dillon," she replied.

"Wow! That is Jeremy's son?" I asked.

"No, but she is about seven months pregnant now," Rose said as she placed her tea on the coffee table.

I touched my belly and replied, "She's pregnant? Really? That is good. Where are they now?" I asked nicely.

"They are in Itta Bena, Mississippi right now. We have folks down there, and Donna took Jeremy to meet some of the family. You know, family time, vacation before the baby comes along and everything," Rose answered.

"Oh, okay," was all I could say. However, unknowingly, Rose continued to rub salt in my wound.

"They are so happy together. You should see them. They are so in love, if I ever did witness love myself. I am so glad that his ex-girlfriend let him go. If she had not, my Donna would not have met him and gained a wonderful man."

"What about his ex-girlfriend?" I asked.

"You know what? Let me call him and let him know that his classmate is here. I know he will kill me for telling his business, the way I have been running my mouth."

She got up and went to the phone. When she picked up the phone receiver, I got the butcher knife out of my purse and said, "I'm the crazy bitch he dumped."

Rose froze, and I put the knife to her neck. "Now Rose, I need to know the address where your daughter and my soon-to-be-husband are. You lie to me, and I will come back and kill you bitch," I threatened.

"Please don't hurt me," Rose pleaded.

"Fuck you. Give me the address. I won't ask you again," I replied.

"It's on the sticker pad, there on the refrigerator," she replied nervously.

I glanced over towards the refrigerator, and there it was in bold letters. I pushed the knife deeper into Rose's neck and said, "Damn, bitch. I didn't know it was going to be that easy. I promise. Your daughter and her baby will join your fucking ass in hell."

Her eyes bucked, and her mouth widened as I sliced and cut the main vein in her neck. She fell, grabbing her neck with her hand, as she tried to run away from me.

I quickly walked up behind her and said, "This was my design Jeremy let your daughter live in. This is my house; my dream your daughter is living."

Rose fell to the floor on her face. I got on her back and picked up her head. Leaning closer to her ear, I said, "Your daughter Donna is going to die, bitch. As for the baby in her stomach, I am going to cut it out and drop it on the floor."

To make sure she bled to death, I cut everywhere I thought a vein was located. I wanted this bitch to die slowly.

I sat on the floor beside Rose's body and cried.

"This is my life your daughter is living. My house, my fantasy, and my husband she is with."

I got up, turned in circles, and screamed as loudly as I possibly could.

"Donna, you will pay. You will pay dearly for stealing Jeremy away from me! Wait until I see you!"

I walked over to the refrigerator. The address on the notepad read 2122 Summers Avenue, Itta Bena, MS. I walked over to the sink and washed the blood from my hands and face. After drying them off, I gathered a pen and some paper from the counter and wrote down the address. I took five hundred dollars in cash that I found in Rose's purse and put it in my pocket. Then I thought, *Why take the money?* I took the whole muther-fucking purse. I checked to see if she had anything else I'd want, but she didn't. I went into the master bedroom. I went through the clothes and took a few of Donna's things. I noticed a jewelry box, and I looked in it. Right before my very eyes was the ring I'd wanted Jeremy to get me. In an instant, my mind took me back at the jewelry store as I talked to Jeremy.

"Jeremy, I would love to have that ring on my finger," I said to him as he asked the clerk to let us see it.

"One day Nicole, I would love to give you that ring but ..."

"I know. I know. We are going to wait and make sure everything is going to be perfect between us," I said cutting him off.

"Right. Nothing but the best for the woman that deserves the best, and the best is with me," Jeremy said as he stared into my eyes.

"Jeremy, I will never stop telling you how happy you make me. Even if I never see the ring again, I am content as long as we are together," I spoke to him with a smile that lit up the room.

I snapped back to reality and the ring. I tried it on and it fit easily on my ring finger. I went back to Donna's clothes. I assumed she could fit all these things before she became swollen with my child. I stole me a couple of outfits that were my size. I was going to love seeing their faces when they saw me in her clothes, and yes, wearing MY ring.

I went back downstairs, dragged Rose's body to the child's room and closed the door. Before I headed out the front door, I hung up the phone and set it up to go to voicemail. I went to the kitchen and put all kinds of snacks, bottles of water and juice into a white plastic bag. I closed the door behind me, got in the driver's seat and began hitting the steering wheel with all my might. I looked up and saw a car with a boy and a girl sitting in it. They looked at me and asked, "Lady, you okay?"

I screamed at them like a mad woman. "Leave me alone, you little muther-fuckers!"

"Screw you lady!" the boy yelled.

"Fuck you, you fucking bastard!" I yelled.

They drove off, and I waited for a few minutes. I realized I needed a new ride, so I decided to get the vehicle out of the garage. I was stunned to see that it was a Toyota Camry. Thankfully, it was full of gas. Something about old folks keeping everything in order made me smile. I opened the glove compartment, took out the map, and scanned over it. I drove out of the garage, stopped at the car I'd stolen earlier and put my shovel and machete in the trunk. I put the knife in the glove compartment, reloaded the 9mm, and stashed it in the purse I'd taken from Rose. It was time I hurried up and got to Jeremy before all those bodies were traced back to me. Luckily, I was moving from state to state at a good pace. Fuck the police; they'd never catch me at this rate. I looked both ways, drove out the driveway and headed towards Jeremy, in Itta Bena, Mississippi.

Chapter 14

As the cool evening air filled the car, I popped an ecstasy pill and perked on up. I turned up the radio and drove as fast as I could. The highway traffic was scarce, and the patrolmen were few. This made it easier for me to ride out without being hassled. However, that wouldn't have mattered to me because the thought of Jeremy and his so-called wife fueled my anger now. If he only knew...now, I was not just mad, but pissed.

Nothing Nicole could say to me would ever make me turn around now. In the beginning, Jeremy had to pay, and now he really had to pay for everything I had been through. He got married to someone that was not me; he has a child on the way not by me; he got my dream house without me, and he even has my child's things in the yard. He is happy, and he is not with me.

The tears were rolling down my face non-stop as the memories of Jeremy surrounded all of my thoughts. *How could he do such a thing to me? I loved him so damn much*, I thought as I drove faster.

"Nicole, talk to me. I need you to talk to me," I said, but Nicole said nothing. I looked in the rearview mirror, and she did not appear. I started driving faster and faster. Nicole still did not appear, so I played chicken with an eighteen-wheeler. Still no Nicole. When I got about thirty feet from the truck the clicking began, and so did Nicole's voice.

"Nikki, watch out!" she yelled, and I moved just in time, running off the road and into a shallow ditch.

"Nikki, calm down and relax. It is going to be okay," Nicole continued.

"How is it going to be okay, when I am pissed and ready to kill Jeremy? He is the reason my life is so fucked up," I said as I hit the steering wheel multiple times.

"Nikki stay focused," Nicole said.

"Voice in my head, have you not noticed that I do not listen to you, like you want me to?" I said.

"Nikki, breathe in and say 'the sun is warm; the grass is green'. Come on. Repeat it."

So I said, "The sun is warm; the grass is green; the sun is warm; the grass is green. Wait. What the fuck is this supposed to do? You have me doing group therapy?" I screamed at Nicole.

"Let me have more control, Nikki. I believe that I can handle my life now," Nicole said to me in a low, still voice, sounding unsure of herself.

"Ha! Nicole, if I let you run things, we both will be caught, and no way will I let you get me fucked up in some more asylum shit. What are you trying to prove by asking to run things?" I asked Nicole.

"I can handle my life now, which is what I am saying. After watching you, I see that I need to be more assertive and more aggressive to get what I need done," Nicole replied nicely to me.

"Hold on bitch. We'll talk about you and your life, but what the fuck does the sun and grass have to do with me and you?" I retorted.

"Nikki, that is just a technique I used to get you to calm down, and not do anything stupid. That's all."

"Do something stupid? What about all this bullshit I have been through because you wouldn't speak the fuck up? Do something stupid? What about finding out where your precious Jeremy is, then find out that he is married with a damn kid on the way? Don't you trust me to take him out?" I screamed.

"If I can't trust you Nikki, who can I trust?" Nicole said harshly to me.

"I don't know, Nicole. Let us see if you trust me," I said.

With the car still in the shallow ditch, I reached inside my purse, grabbed the 9mm and pointed it under the base of her chin and said to the bitch, "What you going to do now, huh? Can you stop me from killing you, huh? Can you? Do you have what it takes to stop me, if need be?"

I waited on an answer, but she did not reply. I removed the gun and placed it back into my purse. Then, Nicole asked, "If you had killed me, how would you get revenge on Jeremy for us?"

I took the knife out of the glove compartment and pointed at the rearview mirror. I aimed it at Nicole in a defensive move, then looked harder in the mirror at the eyes that were a reflection of mine. I realized that she was not moving, so I snatched the car in drive and drove out of the shallow ditch. I drove faster and faster, speeding like a crazy person, a crazy person on a mission.

When I glanced into the mirror hours later, I thought I was going to see Nicole with a smirk on her face; but this time, when I looked into the mirror, blue lights were shining bright and sirens filled my ears. With my head straight and my eyes on the speedometer, I saw that I was speeding. I glanced ahead and noticed that the LEAVING DENVER, COLORADO sign was in view. So, I pulled into the parking lot of this abandoned mom and pop store located near the state sign. The police officer got out, walked over to the car and said, "Ma'am, you were speeding. Do you know how fast you were going?"

"No, sir. I was trying to get away from my ex-husband," I said as I produced fake tears.

"Do you have any ID? If not, I will have to take you downtown," he said nastily.

"No, but I am lonely and in need of a man in uniform to clear my head, if you know what I mean," I said as I pointed my head towards his crotch.

The male cop looked around and said, "Come over to my cruiser. There probably won't be a car coming through here for hours."

Not knowing what to expect, I took my purse and went to the passenger side of his cruiser. I was very nervous, because I knew these bitches had a BOLO out for me. This muther-fucker could be tricking me. If this was a game, he'd better come correct because I wasn't going to go down easy. As I stepped around to the passenger side of the vehicle, in the parking lot of the abandoned mom and pop store, I looked down and saw he had his little-ass dick sticking out. I looked up at him and asked, "Do you have any money? I am in need of some cash, fast. I am trying to run away. Can you help me?"

"Bitch, I can give you a ticket, or better yet, haul you in for trying to fight me. Now, come give me some damn lip service." *Click, click, click*. My head began banging like a mutha.

As I placed my hands on my head, the bitch said loudly in my ears, "Nikki, please don't do anything crazy." To drown out her voice, I put my fingers in my ears and I made a popping sound as my fingers came out. I looked down at his dick and said, "Officer, you are right."

I licked my lips seductively, lowered my head and started giving him head. I wanted to bite that muther-fucker off but decided to suck his dick like he had demanded.

As he was enjoying the pleasure I was giving him, I eased my 9mm out of the purse with my right hand. When I pulled my mouth off him, I looked up at him and said sexily, "You like it, Mr. Officer?"

"Did I tell you to take my dick out your mouth? Take me deep right damn now," he said with rapid breathing caused from the pleasure I was giving him.

I gently went back down on his dick and deep throated him. As I pulled up gently, I said,

"You know, I don't like it when men abuse power, and I hate authority, so enjoy this, Mr. Officer."

He looked down because he felt the cool point of the gun aimed at the base of his dick. Our eyes locked for a few seconds, and, before he could stop me, I pulled the trigger. Blood went everywhere. I pulled my head up higher and saw that my face, hands, and fingers were covered in blood. I wiped them on his shirt and sat upright in the seat. I turned my head to the left and saw that he was slouched over the steering wheel and not moving. I assumed he was dead and for sure, dead with no muther-fucking dick.

I got out the car with my purse draped over my right shoulder. I opened the driver's side door and pushed him over to the passenger side. I looked at his slumped body as his head leaned towards the window and said loudly, "I'm the last bitch to bust your nut, and it was a good one too, you fucking pig." I got in the car and began reaching for his wallet. He grabbed my right hand with his left hand and I snapped the fuck out.

"Oh, you're not dead? Let me help you to the grave."

Using my right hand, I took my knife out the purse, and I stabbed and grinded it into his genital area in a circular motion. He was still grabbing at me, trying to hit me. I looked at him and said, "Now, deep throat this you fucking maggot."

That was when I jammed the knife into his throat until he moved no more. "Go to hell, pig, and tell them who helped you out."

I sat back and watched for more movement from him. It was astounding to see a man blow bubbles out of his neck as I witnessed him take his last breath of life. To make sure he was gone, I felt for a pulse. "I wish those bitches would give you a medal of honor for dying in the line of duty," I laughed out loud. I picked up his wallet and saw a picture of his family—two kids and a pregnant wife.

"Girl, I did you a damn favor. Now, raise your kids to be real men," I joked.

I threw the picture onto his bloody body and checked out his cash. It was low, but I took all he had anyway. I placed the car into drive and began riding until I found a spot to hide the car out of sight. I got out and went back to the trunk of the Camry. I opened the bag I had the clothes in, got out a towel and poured sanitizer on it. I stripped off my clothes, wiped the blood away from my face, hands, and hair. I eyed a revealing piece of clothing in the bag, so I pulled it out. It was a beautiful sun dress. Honestly, it was a dress that reminded me of the one Jeremy had bought me years earlier, so I put it on.

I yawned as I began to feel the pill wearing off. I closed the trunk and climbed into the driver's side of the car. I let the seat back and went to sleep with Jeremy on my mind.

"I love you, Nicole. I love only you Nicole. You are my best friend, you know that?" Jeremy said to me as he held my hand while we walked on the beach.

"We have been a beautiful couple for such a long time, and we fit so perfectly together, don't you agree?" I said to Jeremy.

"Nicole, I — " was all I heard Jeremy say.

As I looked up at the sky, I didn't get a chance to hear him actually say I love you. I didn't understand why he couldn't love me as he loved his wife. He met this lady and married her. Why am I not worthy? I closed my eyes and tried to rest.

My mind began to wander. With no warning at all, the sunny day at the beach got dark, and the wind blew fiercely. No one was on the beach but me. I looked up, and the ocean waves were very high. On the ledge, I saw Jeremy. He was wearing a white tux, and I spoke to him softly, "Jeremy, wait! Don't marry her. She will never love you like I do. Jeremy, make me your wife. Make me the one to share your life with. Not her. Don't marry her. No, Jeremy."

When I awoke hours later, my arms were stretched out, and I was calling on Jeremy. I wiped my eyes and nervously opened my purse. I grabbed the upper and took it. I closed my eyes, and allowed the pill to go through my system. I opened my eyes again, put the key in the ignition and drove off. More hours passed, and I made it to Wichita, KS. The area was different, and the people seemed more closed up.

"This is better. I don't have to worry about them being all in my face, trying to figure out who I am and so forth," I thought. I stopped at the first convenience store I found, gassed up and stole the change in the register. I walked out the store and saw a woman and a child by my car as the gas pumped. The mother looked at me and asked, "Can you watch my son while I go in? I don't want to take him out the booster seat just so I can pay for gas. I promise I won't be long in the store. What ya say? Can you watch him for a few minutes for me?"

I looked at her, then back at the child as he looked out the back driver side window and replied, "Yeah, but hurry up. I have shit to do."

"Thank you, miss. I'll be right out," she said as she walked towards the store in a hurry, trusting me with her child. I was a stranger, but it seemed like she didn't give a damn.

When she went inside, the little boy looked at me and said, "You that crazy lady on TV." Taken by surprised, I went to his side of the SUV, opened the door where he was and looked at him. Seeing that my far off look did nothing to him, I placed my face closer to his, and in a deep hatred filled voice, I said, "If you tell anyone who I am, I will have to kill you, and I'm sure you are not ready to die, you little fucker."

He replied to me with a smirk on his little pie face. "I ain't scared of you, crazy lady. I'll tell my daddy to kill you."

I looked at this kid. He couldn't be any more than six years old. *He can talk good for his age and can remember shit. I might have to take him and his mama out. What the fuck?*

When I made sure his mother could not see me, I grabbed the little boy under his neck, making him gasp for air. I choked him until he was unconscious. I let his body fall back into the booster seat. Then, I went back to the driver's side of my car and waited for his mother to come out. When she appeared, I said, "He went to sleep so fast."

"Wow, I didn't know he was sleepy," she said in a surprised tone before she pumped her gas.

I responded as I walked off, "I didn't know he was sleepy either, little fucking bastard."

I drove off and rode for more hours than I would have normally. When I began to feel weak and tired, I started drinking energy drinks and colas back to back. When those wore off, I would down the twelve hour No-Doze tablets because I had to get to Mississippi ASAP. I drove faster and farther than ever. I knew that taking a lot of breaks would only prolong my intentions, and there was no way in hell that I was going to allow Nicole a chance to resurface. The more I drove, the more I cried. The tears would come without stopping. I would wipe them away, and still they would fall.

With each tear that fell, I felt more depressed and down about Jeremy not being in my life. Somehow, my mind would not allow me to grasp the idea that he was married and had a baby on the way. He had stepped out on me, and I was going to make that bastard pay for all the heartache and pain he'd caused me. To be honest, I was going to do it for all the women in the world who had had a man pull their hearts out of their chests and walk on them. I just couldn't let that shit ride, not after all I had done just to find him. I had to make my mark, and I would do so with a bang.

I didn't remember passing through any of the small towns, but I was happy to see the sign that read WELCOME TO DALLAS, TEXAS. The city was bustling with cars and tall buildings; however, everything about the cities in the south felt more like a home I never had. As I drove farther out of the city, my stomach began to growl. I happened to look around and noticed a lonely man diner. Since I was hungry, I drove to the partially lit diner off the I-20 exit. *Click, click, click*. The bitch was back.

"What do you want bitch? Every time you show up, some shit goes down," I said to her.

"Go to the bathroom and tape a knife to the middle of your back," Nicole ordered.

"Bitch, what you talking about?" I asked.

She only replied, "Listen to me for once."

Not feeling like putting up with her mess, I obeyed and then found the nearest table. I sat there with my head down thinking, because every time she talked to me, my head ached.

While there I ordered a waffle, coffee, and a side of bacon, and I had the instinct that someone was watching me. I peeped up from eating and saw a small middle aged white man watching me. He was bald, fat and not all that good-looking, so I continued to ignore him. The man kept on looking at me until I could no longer eat. I finally decided to make sure he was interested, so I nodded my head, and as I expected, he nodded back. I called the waitress over and told her that the gentleman at the end of the bar would be picking up the tab. She went over to him, and he handed her the money. Moments later, he came over to me and sat down.

I smiled, and he said, "If you aren't the prettiest thing ever, so why are you here alone?"

"Did you see anyone come in with me when I arrived?" I asked as I stared into his face.

"An aggressive woman? I like that. Are you married? Do you have kids?" he asked.

"No. No, I do not have children. Why? Do you?" I asked, trying to size him up, because he did not look like the type to pick up women.

"Yes, I have six children with my wife," he said in a funny way.

How many others do you have? I thought. When he said wife, I looked up at him and asked, "What's wrong? You don't love her or something?" I asked him softly.

"I do love her," he said. After a short pause, he said, "She used to be my best friend. I had broken it off with her before, but I took her back, even though she can be a little coo-coo. If you know what I mean?"

"What do you mean by a 'little coo-coo'?" I asked him.

"Just like I said, but I guess you can say that, after having all those kids, things began to go south with the marriage."

"Things went south? How so?" I asked him in a nice way.

"She lost her figure, and all she does is nag. I built her the house we had designed when we were younger, and I am the one who is not happy." Holding up my hands, I stopped him from talking because he was doing the same thing to his wife that Jeremy had done to me.

"Let me get this right. You want someone to play with because your wife is fat and talks too much?" I asked dryly.

"Right," he answered.

"You also said she was your best friend. You bought her the dream house you both designed, and now you believe she is coo-coo because she nags you?"

"Right," he said again.

"What makes her crazy? If you don't mind me asking," I said earnestly, then waited on his response.

"When I tried to break it off with her, she started begging me to stay. I fucked the shit out of her, then told her to leave. I wanted to piss in her face, but I came before I could," he said, laughing. He continued, "The next day, I called her to come back and she came, like a damn fool. But enough about the wife, how about you and I?"

He was going to piss in her face, and he fucked the shit out of her, just like Marvin had done to me. I saw the devious look in his eyes and thought, *What a pleasure it's going to be to kill you.*

With a nod of my head, I got up and went to the ladies' room. He followed me, and we met up at the restroom doors.

"You look like you are in need of a real man to fuck you," he said.

"No, I don't need a man. I need money. Tell me. Do you have any?" I asked.

He opened his wallet and showed me hundreds of dollars. He even flipped out a few cards. My eyes got big. I could barely contain myself as my eyes lit up at the sight of the money. He saw me drooling, so he quickly closed the wallet in my face. I looked up at his face, and he gave me an ugly expression. I went to the back of the diner and waited for him to come. When he came, I said, "Take off your shirt. I need to see that there are no hidden bugs on you. I can't afford to go to jail on some bullshit."

The man took off his shirt right then and there. I had him to turn around to make sure he had a bare back, which he did. He walked in the men's bathroom, and before I followed him, I got an old sign I had seen in the corner that said UNDER CONSTRUCTION and put it on the door. Once inside, I locked it, and to make sure that I would not get any blood on my pretty dress, I took it off. His eyes raked my body, and to me, he was no better than Marvin and Jeremy.

He sat on the floor, and I knew that would make my job easier. I placed my purse by the sink and sat on him. His dick was small, so I was going to have to work at this shit. His dick was not pleasing looking, so I made up my mind to play him. I sat on the small dick man, but his dick was limp. I sat on him anyway. He had his eyes closed, and he really thought he was in me. In the middle of it, I stopped and said, "Fat man, pussy kills," as I took the knife from the middle of my back quickly. I plunged it into his chest cavity. I tried to break bones and tear tissue. I dug the knife deep into him and cut him open. His eyes were glued on me, and his body shook and shook as I sat there. As he tried to rise up, I realized his dick had gotten hard. It felt like it was much bigger than what I had seen at first.

"Damn, I need to get a quick nut," I said out loud while looking at his face.

I began to move up and down, trying to ride his dick before it went down. Within minutes, I nutted on that nearly dead muther-fucker. I stood up and wiped the sweat off my eyebrow. I looked down and saw that his dick was limp again.

"Damn, muther-fucker! Your dick is limp as a fucking noodle," I said.

I looked into his face. I used my right hand and struggled to take out his heart. When I did feel the soft, small tissue beating, I yanked it forcefully. He looked at my hand and saw his heart and for a few seconds, we watched the heart beat in my hand. His body jerked once more and his hands fell flat. "Pussy ass muther-fucker, you're just like the rest of them."

I tried to drag his body to the bathroom stall. Since he was fat, this bitch was like a ton of bricks. I moved his body little by little until I got him up near one of the toilets. Thinking that people would be coming in, I decided to leave him in the stall since I couldn't lift him up on the toilet. I took the money from his wallet inside his jacket and threw his clothes in the garbage can near the sink. I cleaned up my hands and put paper towels on the blood. As I washed my hands and face, my head began aching. *Click, click, click*. The fucking noises again. This shit was sounding louder and louder. I grabbed the sink with both of my hands and gritted my teeth as I saw Nicole smiling at me in the mirror.

"Put your clothes on and leave," she said.

"Are you helping me?" I asked, puzzled. This was the first time I'd asked her something without cursing her out.

"No, it is not just about you. I want to live, Nikki, and, before you know it, I will be the one stopping you, not Jeremy, not the police, but me," Nicole spoke with a little bass in her voice.

"Bitch, I am not so sure about that," I said.

"Not sure about what Nikki?" she asked.

"Not sure about you stopping me. You are not strong enough to stop fleas from flying around your ass. Stopping me will be a job that I know you are not strong enough to complete," I said to her, and she stopped talking. Just like I thought; a weak ass bitch.

I finished washing up and put my dress back on. I grabbed my purse and walked out the restroom unnoticed and undetected. I got back into the car, drank another energy drink and peeled the fuck out.

Hours passed, and I was getting tired again. I stopped in Monroe, Louisiana. I went to the Wal-Mart off the interstate and took a brief nap in the parking lot.

The dreams began, and this time, I had a gun on Jeremy. He looked so afraid, but before I could pull the trigger, out of the corner of my eye, I saw that weak-ass Cowboy, swinging a shovel. A loud sound was all I remembered. I jumped up out of my sleep and screamed out loud, “Cowboy!”

I looked in the mirror and knew that I had to pay Cowboy a visit before I saw Jeremy and his wife. Cowboy’s little pussy ass would pay for what he did. He was the main reason why I got caught. He was going to wish that he never knew me.

I popped a No-Doze, drank an energy drink, cranked the car up and drove off. I sped, faster than ever. It took everything I had not to get angry, but that shit wasn’t happening. Now, my plan was to find Cowboy and make him pay for knocking me the fuck out. *Click*. “Not now.” *Click*. “Stop it.” *Click*. “Leave me alone.”

“Bitch I am pissed off, so you better have some good shit to tell me. If not, keep the shit to your damn self,” I told Nicole before she got started with her sad-ass story.

“Nikki, you have my permission to do what you must,” Nicole replied calmly.

“I really don’t need your permission to do a muther-fucking thing. He had them put me in Raymond Neil. That hell hole was pathetic and not fit for anyone. That weak ass Cowboy hit me. I remember now, he knocked the fuck out of me, and he spoiled my plans with Jeremy.

“You stupid bitch, what the hell did he hit me for any damn way?” I continued.

“He wanted to do right. It is a moral thing, Nikki. You don’t have any morals,” Nicole said.

"Morals will get a bitch fucked up, and if you show your feelings, you allow a muther-fucker to gut you. Now, that is something I plan not to do, for if I did, I would end up like you— weak."

"I'm not weak Nikki. I want us back together as one. You seem to have forgotten who loves you, who cares for you, and dammit, who created you," Nicole shot back.

"You fucking bitch, I know you aren't throwing this bullshit up in my face. I fucking love you girl. That's why I'm out here looking for Jeremy— all because you want to see him. I'm doing this for you bitch," I yelled.

"Stop lying to your damn self Nikki. You're trying to kill Jeremy. This is because of you. I love that nigga, and you want to kill him, but over my dead body."

"You fucking bitch, I can arrange that shit. Your dead body is all I need. Then, I can live in muther-fucking peace."

"Nikki, you are taking this too far. You have killed so many people because you're pissed off. I'm pissed too, but I'm not killing."

"Shut the fuck up muther-fucker! You are the main one who wanted me to kill those bitches about Jeremy. You wanted them gone, and I did that. Give me some fucking credit," I spoke angrily.

"It's true. I wanted them dead, but I didn't want to kill them. You did that," Nicole agreed.

"Bitch, I'm tired of talking to you. You are really beginning to get on my damn nerves. Just hope I don't try to take you out the muther-fucking game. I'm so tired of you nagging me. Just remember that all this is because I love you. That's why Jeremy must pay," I explained.

Nicole didn't say another word to me. She knew that I was right. All these killings were on her. I killed for her love for Jeremy. Every time I turned around, it was Jeremy this and Jeremy that. I was so tired of that worthless piece of shit. He was just like a thorn I couldn't seem to get from underneath my skin. Nicole was hurt and didn't know what the fuck she wanted. I was there to tell her what the fuck she wanted and needed. I was her fucking boss; she was not my boss. Nicole continued to shut the fuck up as I drove for hours in silence.

Chapter 15

WELCOME TO MISSISSIPPI was the most beautiful sign I had ever seen. I never thought I would love coming down there again, but for revenge, I was willing to do anything. With those welcoming words, I knew that revenge was a few hours away somewhere, but here all the same. I drove around in town and came to the conclusion that things hadn't changed since I'd last been there with Jeremy. I drove deeper into the empty, rundown town and was eager to get out. I was not going to leave until I accomplished what I needed to do. However, how I couldn't wait for Cowboy to see my face. To me, his look would be worth the risk of getting caught. The look on his big hog-ass face would be priceless.

It was morning again, and at this time of day, he would be going to work soon. I needed to act fast if I planned on surprising the man who had surprised me. Finding his place was not hard at all because one thing I had learned about being with a man was that they don't change much.

I chose a more secluded place to park the car because I had to be careful. Even though this was a small town, these are some nosy muther-fuckers in Mississippi. When I had stayed there with Cowboy, the neighbors were always out and watching everything. If someone came and you were gone, they would tell you who came, what they wanted, what they had on and which direction they went. We never had to lock our doors or anything like that, because the people always gave a new meaning to neighborhood watch.

I looked at everyone. I had to lay low because they never forgot a face. My hair was different, but I was sure that if one of those nosey muther-fuckers saw me, I would have to kill them. That would not be a problem, but I was there for one person and one person only. However, if any others got in the way, I would do what I had to do. I wouldn't have minded taking all those bitches out.

Cowboy was smart and paid great attention to his surroundings; therefore, I had to be careful. He would notice the slightest thing, and if I messed up, taking him out would be more than a job for me to do. He was a fat boy, and I didn't want to do more than what I had to.

People were not stirring, so getting my weapons was not a problem. I decided on a small wooden baseball bat and the machete. While acting normal, I continued walking towards Cowboy's place. I turned the door knob and laughed because he still left the door unlocked. He'd once said that thieving people would expect you to have your door locked, and he was not afraid of anyone.

I entered his home, closed the door firmly and gazed around. I saw some binoculars, so I placed them in my purse. I figured they would come in handy in the future. I went on into the living room and placed my items on the couch. I observed the area and saw this big, beautiful Queen Anne bed with poles. He did have a little taste after all. I looked to the left and saw a lot more beautiful things that I liked. His taste was sort of like mine, except for all the pigs, cows, and horses he had around here. I didn't like animals. He claimed he was a real cowboy, but was more like a nasty-ass cow.

I headed to the kitchen because I had gotten hungry again. I viewed the items in his fridge and got out some Chinese food and warmed it up in the microwave. I sat down and began eating. *It wasn't too bad here*, I thought as I ate the food hungrily. When I finished eating, I put the empty container back in the fridge, in the same place I got it from. I pushed my chair back to the table and went to retrieve my purse, but I left the machete and wooden bat on the couch. I walked slowly because, although this place had been a safe place for me in the beginning, that was then. I didn't know whether the police were looking for me here too.

I opened the door to his bedroom and was not surprised. His bed was made up, and it smelled nice. I walked over to his closet, pulled out a shirt, and went to the bathroom. He had Dove body wash. *How odd*, I thought as I picked up the body wash. I enjoyed the water on my body as the scent of lilac covered me.

After my shower, I put on his shirt and wrapped my arms around my body. *Click, click, click* went the clacking in my head.

"Nicole, before you say anything, I want to say that since you warned me at the diner, I will allow you a short memory."

I closed my eyes, and when I opened them again, Nicole saw herself in the mirror. She saw how she'd looked before Nikki took form. Nicole was relieved.

"Close your mind to everything but the sound of my voice," I said to Nicole.

"Can't you feel Jeremy's arms around you? Holding you ever so close?" Nikki continued in a low, sweet voice.

Without giving Nikki a verbal answer, I kept my eyes closed and visualized Jeremy holding me. The smile on my face was as huge as the Grand Canyon. I twirled around as if my love Jeremy was dancing with me and his arms held me tenderly. For over twenty minutes, I danced with the happy thoughts of Jeremy in my heart, not paying attention to Nikki. I danced and danced until I got close to the purse. With swiftness, I opened up the purse and took out the gun, but before I could pull the trigger, Nikki knocked my right hand away, and the shot rang out, tearing a medium-sized hole in Cowboy's bedroom wall.

"You stupid muther-fucking bitch! I give you an inch, and you try to take a mile. What the fuck?" Nikki said angrily as she put the gun away.

"I'm the only damn friend you have, and you want to fuck me up. What the hell is wrong with you, bitch? You have tried this dumb shit before! Next time, I won't let that shit slide too easily," Nikki continued.

"Nikki, before I let you continue to take out innocent people, I will do what I have to do to take you out. Is that clear?" Nicole said, for the first time, with hatred in her tone.

"You weak bitch, you growing balls now? You are growing them with the wrong fucking one. Don't you know that I will fuck your world up? Flip that bitch inside out and strip it to muther-fucking pieces? Don't you ever try to take me out again 'cause, if you do, I will do more than kill Jeremy. I will start killing children and helpless babies. Now get that shit clear, take your ass to sleep and leave me the fuck alone. I have a damn job to do, and I can't do it if I am worried about you trying to pull some hoe shit like you did today."

I looked in the mirror again and saw my reflection. I turned around, got on Cowboy's bed and went to sleep with murder on my mind and thoughts of how to keep that bitch Nicole out of my way.

I woke up feeling well rested. It was now three P.M. and Cowboy should have been home around seven P.M. I went over to the couch to make sure my machete and bat were still there. I gathered them up and decided to hide them under Cowboy's bed. My plans were to cook a huge dinner, fuck him until his dick was sore, and then kill that muther-fucker off. He deserved to die for getting me caught.

I went to the kitchen and prepared a big supper. I cooked him mashed potatoes, Southern fried chicken, green beans, corn on the cob, and apple cobbler for dessert. To top it off, I brewed some Southern sweet tea. Cowboy was going to love this grand "homecoming" that I had planned for him, but first, I had to convince this fool that I had been released from that fucking nut house.

"Damn, I need something to help me out," I said out loud.

"Look in his medicine cabinet," Nicole suggested.

"OMG, Nicole! I can't believe you are helping me. I'm so proud of you," I replied.

"I'm just giving you an idea because Cowboy was the reason we got caught," she explained.

"You damn right! I'm so glad you're finally beginning to see this shit my way," I replied as I made my way to his bedroom to look around for some type of medicine. I needed this bitch to die a slow death. He'd ruined my life, and now I would take his life.

I searched through his bathroom and found a lot of medicine under the sink in a small clear container. I fumbled through the shit and found some Benadryl and a pill bottle filled with Hydrocodone. Damn, I was happier than a gay man with a big bag of colorful dicks of all shapes and sizes. I took both bottles and went back into the kitchen. I finely crushed up eight pills of Hydrocodone and poured them into the mashed potatoes. Then, I poured in half a bottle of Benadryl and mixed it together. I prayed that both the Benadryl and Hydrocodone would help me bring him down. He is a big boy, and I needed a little help.

As I sat at the table, I heard Cowboy pull up. I ran to the window and saw him looking at my car. I jumped up and down like a kid in a candy store. I took off running out the front door, and Cowboy jumped around like someone was after him.

"Hello Cowboy! I'm so glad you are home," I said as I gave him a big hug.

"Nicole," he replied with a dumbfounded look on his face.

"Yes, it's me in the flesh," I said.

"Wow, I didn't know that you were out," he said with his mouth still open.

"Oh yes! They released me a couple of days ago. And I wanted to come to Mississippi and make things right with you. All those terrible things I did in the past were sad, but I'm better now and trying to get my life together," I lied with a straight face.

"Is that right?" he responded in a more relaxed tone.

"Yes baby. I thought about you loving me, and I wanted to make things right with us. Is that okay or shall I leave?" I said in a sad tone.

"No, Nicole. I have no other woman. Damn girl! I'm so glad that you're better. I've been thinking about you a lot lately," Cowboy replied.

"Really? Well, come on in because I have cooked you a big supper," I said.

"Supper?" he replied as he stopped in his tracks.

"Yes, supper. Is that okay with you? I didn't mean to invade your privacy. I thought you would be happy to know that I'm all better and wondered if you wanted a life with me as I do with you," I sadly murmured with puppy dog eyes.

"Hell yeah! I do," his big country ass replied.

Cowboy and I hugged up and went inside the house. Before he ate, he wanted to get in the shower. He stripped off his clothes and entered the shower. As the water ran, I had a short conversation with him. Then, it hit me to get in the shower with him. I took off my clothes and entered the shower. Cowboy jumped as I opened the shower doors. "Damn, why

are you so nervous? I told you that I'm all better. They released me. You act like I escaped or something," I joked.

"I apologize, baby," he replied.

As the water hit my body, Cowboy got down on his knees and began licking on my pussy. It seemed like his tongue was fatter or my pussy was hotter. Whichever it was, I didn't want him to stop. After a few minutes; I moved him back and got on my knees to suck his big, long-ass dick. He leaned against the shower wall as I caressed both my hands on his dick and began sucking. I teased him by licking the head and then taking him deeper into my mouth. I sucked and sucked until I thought it was time for him to cum. I figured he would have busted a nut by now, but he surprised me.

He lifted me up, turned me around and bent me over. He stuck his tongue deeper into my pussy before entering me. He worked his huge dick in inch by inch. I began thrusting back on him as he pushed forward. We stroked and stroked and stroked like no tomorrow. Within minutes, he took out his dick and nutted on my ass as the water hitting my back washed it off. He stuck it back inside me. Cowboy was hard again and was fucking me like he had just broken out of prison. As I closed my eyes, he turned the water off. He pulled out of me, lifted me up and carried me to the bed. We both were still dripping wet, but he placed me on the bed anyway. He pulled me to the edge of the bed and began ramming my pussy. I placed my legs on his shoulders as he held my thighs while pounding away at me. I moaned and groaned with happiness. After about thirty minutes, he came all over my stomach. He jumped down on

the floor and ate my pussy until I came in his mouth. He licked and licked until I was completely satisfied.

"Damn, that was a good welcome home present," I said breathlessly.

"I want you to be satisfied and happy," he replied.

"Thank you. I'm very happy. Now, we can go eat dinner."

"That's right. I'm very hungry," he agreed.

"Well, let me go fix my man a big meal," I replied as I got off the bed and headed to the kitchen naked. Cowboy followed right behind me, naked also. He sat down at the kitchen table and I warmed everything up. I fixed him a huge plate and placed it in front of him. Cowboy had two plates of mashed potatoes, six pieces of fried chicken, three corn on the cobs, no green beans, and about four glasses of sweet tea. I laughed as this muther-fucking fool gobbled all that shit down. I ate two pieces of chicken, green beans, and a piece of apple pie. It would have been crazy of me to eat the rest of the shit.

Cowboy sat at the table for a few minutes. When he began to look crazy, I asked, "What's wrong with you?"

"Don't know, but I feel funny as hell," he replied.

"How do you feel funny?" I asked.

"I feel groggy or something," he slurred.

"Do you feel groggy, or do you feel drugged up?" I asked while laughing.

He laughed too. It was as if he was very high. I got up from the table and proceeded to the bedroom to retrieve the baseball bat. As I reached under the bed and pulled out the bat, I could hear him coming down the hall. I stood next to the door and waited for him to enter. As soon as his foot crossed the threshold, I knocked him the fuck out, just the way he had done me. I hit him two more times, then dragged his fat ass down the hall. I had to struggle for almost thirty minutes to get him to the living room, as the blood made a trail. Once I got his heavy ass away from the door, I stretched him out and began his punishment.

I picked up the bat and put it on the couch. Then, I got the machete from under the bed and began slicing and dicing, making small cuts all over his body. He woke up and started hollering, "Nicole, please!" I wasn't afraid of him getting up and attacking me because he was too drugged up on Hydrocodone and Benadryl. His tears seemed real, and when he saw me coming closer to him, Cowboy began scooting backwards.

I started taunting him as he tried to get away from me.

"I can't hear you, Cowboy. Come closer, so you can stand up to me. How about shaking my hand, like you Mississippi people say, as a right hand of fellowship?"

"Please Nicole! Don't do this. I'm so sorry. Please, Nicole," he begged.

"'Please, Nicole' is not what I want to fucking hear. My name is Nikki. Who the fuck is, Nicole? You have ruined my life and caused me to be locked down like a caged animal. What the fuck was wrong with you? You didn't give a fuck about me then, so why should I care about you now?"

"You were wrong for doing what you did to that boy. He didn't deserve it," Cowboy explained.

"Wrong? Do you know what that boy did to me? He hurt me, and nobody hurts me and gets away with it," I said.

"Nicole, I apologized for what I did," Cowboy pleaded as he winced with pain.

"Nicole? If you call me her name again, I will cut your balls off and put them in your mouth. Now, are you going to explain why you called the FBI on me?" I asked.

"They were already following you, and when I saw that boy down in the cellar after you went to sleep, I called them. I apologize," he begged as he lifted one hand in the air.

Before he could take it down, I swiftly cut his mutherfucking hand off. Cowboy looked down at his hand as it hit the floor and screamed like a little bitch.

"Fuck you Cowboy. You saved Jeremy's life. Let's see if you can save your own life. I'm going to fuck you up, bitch. You will always remember who Nikki is. Believe that," I threatened.

I finished taunting him with hurtful words. Then, I moved closer to him and lifted the machete. He held out his left arm as if to block me, but he underestimated the power of a sharp blade because his arm fell off. His body fell over as he began pleading, "Please Nikki! Don't do this! Please!"

But I paid no attention to him. I looked at his shoulder, from where the arm once hung and told him, "Damn! I'm good. That was a clean chop."

After I spoke those words, I gave him a clean cut across the chest. Then, I stood over him and cut the other arm completely off his body. It comically jumped around like a fish out of water.

"You hateful bitch!" he mumbled.

"Hateful? I'm just an angry bitch. You have really pissed me off, and I'm going to show you just how pissed off I am. I have dreamed of the day I would fuck you up. After I kill you, I'm going to kill Jeremy. You muther-fuckers have really underestimated me, but I will show you," I said as I listened to him moan and groan.

I lowered my machete and thought about what he'd said. Fuck it! I needed to move on to what I came to do. I looked into Cowboy's face, and anger filled my heart. I chopped and chopped at his legs until they both came off. He was sobbing heavily as his blood soaked into the carpet. I went over to his arms and chopped them up into four pieces. His arms were the main thing I wanted to chop up since he'd used those bitches to hit me.

All I could hear in my ears was "God help me. Forgive me for my sins." I looked around and saw Cowboy trying to talk to God. After I finished severing his limbs from the joints, I said to him, "That day you knocked me out, you should have stayed the fuck out my business, but you had to be a fucking hero."

I stood up, drew my machete and continued, "Now, Mr. Big Bad Ass Hero, here's your damn reward." I kicked and kicked him until his body turned over onto his stomach. I took the machete and chopped and chopped at his back, what was left of his legs, and gave one swift chop to the back of his head. Then, I threw the machete on the couch. I turned Cowboy over and began stomping and stomping his muther-fucking head. Then, I kicked what was left of his body. All my anger turned into rage. After about five minutes, I became a little tired.

I sat down on the couch to rest. I picked up the machete and just stared at it. It brought back the memory of when Cowboy had fucking hit me in the back of the head. I remember *running out the front door, throwing up everywhere. My head was spinning like a muther-fucker. The cellar doors were open, and it seemed like they were moving back and forward. My only thought was that this couldn't be happening to me. I stood there for a few seconds trying to focus on the cellar doors. Trying to gather myself, I ran down the stairs, and there was Jeremy standing tall. He was unshackled. No chains. No handcuffs. He stared at me as I looked at him*. I will never forget the look on that nigga's face. I still can't believe that I froze up like a little bitch. *I lifted the gun and shot that pussy ass muther-fucker in the shoulder. He yelled out like the weak bitch he was, but, before I could finish, I looked up into this picture on the wall and saw a reflection of that pussy punk Cowboy. Before I could turn around and shoot him, he hit me in the back of the head, knocking me unconscious.*

That memory played over and over in my head. This weak bitch had to suffer more. I can't just kill this muther-fucker off. I looked at his body; he was barely breathing. My mind began to think. This punk ass Cowboy had a garden. There was a possibility of him having some lye around. I jumped up and ran out to his barn.

I searched and searched, and I finally found half a bag of lye in the small storage room in the barn. I carried the bag of lye back to the house and placed it in the front bathroom. I stopped up the tub and filled it halfway. Then, I returned to the living room and looked down at Cowboy. To my surprise, his eyes were open. I looked closely at his chest for his heartbeat; it was barely moving up and down. I ran back to the tub of hot water. I poured the lye in there, and it began to bubble. I tossed the empty bag to the side and saw a jar sitting on the sink. I filled the jar with the mixture from the tub and walked back to the living room. I squatted down next to Cowboy; I opened his mouth and poured it in. His mouth foamed with white shit running out, and his head jerked from side to side. I jumped back and exclaimed, "Damn, didn't know it was going to do that."

I laughed at the sight of that shit eating away at Cowboy's mouth and eyeballs. I picked up the machete. I looked down at him and placed both of my hands on the sword. I swung, and, with one smooth cracking of his neck, Cowboy's head was decapitated from his body. I took my foot, kicked it in the kitchen and laughed some more. I began chopping that bitch to pieces. My anger was so great towards him. After chopping his torso to pieces, I carried it piece by piece and put it in the tub. I kept his arms and legs for something else. I stood there for quite a while until the lye ate through his body parts. I got tired of watching that boring shit and went back to the living room.

I took my time, stood each limb up and stripped the flesh from it. *How interesting it is to see human flesh being removed from the bone,* I thought as his flesh fell in a huge pile. I went into his utility room and, yes, he still had it. In the corner was a huge meat grinder that he used when he killed wild game. I rolled the machine to the edge of the table, so when I took off pieces I could dispose of it without having to walk too far. Being a fat ass, cornbread, country muther-fucker and all, he always made his own meat, but today, I would be making him my own meat. "Now, that is some funny shit," I said as I put the flesh off his arms and legs into the meat grinder.

Moments later, I was bedazzled at the sight. His flesh actually looked like potted meat. I laughed my ass off at the thought of that sneaky muther-fucker looking like potted meat. I turned my attention back to the rest of his arms and legs that lay on the table. I picked up his head, wiped his mouth and kissed his lips. I caressed his face because many nights he'd helped me through a rough patch, but that shit ended when he hit me upside the muther-fucking head. I grabbed his head by the hair and walked about four feet away from the grinder. I kissed his lips one more time, then threw his head.

As if I was playing on a basketball court, I threw his head into the grinder and scored.

"Yes! Two points for Nikki!" I screamed out as I turned the grinder back on.

However, the joy didn't last. I got bored with cutting the fuck out of Cowboy, so I decided to just put what was left in the huge grinder. I said, "1-2-3, here we go with this pussy ass Cowboy down the meat grinder."

Cowboy's body parts were in two huge plastic containers. I went back to his bedroom and took off his bloody shirt, took a long shower in his bathroom, and put on my sundress, for Jeremy must see me looking my best.

I went back to the kitchen, picked up Cowboy's ground up body, opened the door, and walked outside. I took the containers with me because some cats were nearby. I began feeding them a real Cowboy meal. As I poured him out to the animals, I saw a finger, but one of the cats got it and ran before I could grab it. He had a couple of big hogs in a pen, so I fed them also. Then, I gave a little to them shit-eating dogs that was running around. I sat there for a few minutes watching the hogs slop up Cowboy's remains. I laughed and laughed like someone was tickling me.

"Nikki, you are so bad," I said to myself.

"You are bad, Nikki. I will be so glad when they catch you and lock you down like an animal," Nicole spoke harshly.

"Bitch, I don't give a fuck. They will lock the both of us up. You in this too, muther-fucker," I laughed. She didn't say another word, but I didn't give a fuck.

I got ready to leave. I looked around and saw that the cat was eating his owner's finger. I threw the rest of Cowboy's body on the neighbor's flowers. I picked up my weapons and left before someone called the police.

"Fuck Cowboy! Ol' fat bitch. I bet he regrets the day he double crossed me. Stupid muther-fucker."

Chapter 16

I was finally in Itta Bena, Mississippi. I had never been to this place before, but something about it screamed, "You've got to be fucking kidding me." I drove around the small town and wondered. *Why in the hell would someone want to live all the way out here? There is not shit to do,* I thought as I looked up, expecting to see Nicole, but I didn't. She had been hidden ever since our last conversation back at Cowboy's house. It was amazing to me that I still had this weak muther-fucker around. She was lucky I didn't just kill her off. I was trying to be patient with her, but she was making it hard for a bitch.

Driving around proved to be great because I found the address with no problem, but it was not what I expected. I parked the car near the rundown house and got out the binoculars. There was a woman, sitting on the front porch, looking as pregnant as ever. I took that to be Donna. Her hair blew as the wind made gentle breezes upon the earth. Her breasts were huge with baby milk that gave them their form, and her belly was swollen and full of baby. *My baby,* I thought as anger formed inside of me. A tear escaped from my eye.

I wiped it and said, "No mercy bitch. No mercy."

I looked towards the house again, and there he was. Jeremy was as handsome as ever. His body was rich from the muscles that stood out on him, with those arms that once held Nicole, and with plenty of room to hold a woman twice his size. However, my heart skipped beats at the mere sight of him. I wanted to run over and let him know that his love was back. Now, we could finally be together as one, just like we had planned. *Click, click, click.* My head banged out of control.

"Nikki, I know you want him to die after all he has done to me, but I desire for him to make it out alive. Since you have been real in my life, I have come to terms with forgiveness. I have come to terms with the fact that Jeremy has moved on. It hurts, but I will live, and so will you. I will stop you by all means necessary," Nicole said as if I was not listening to her. I had to let her know from the jump.

"Bitch, don't you know that I can hear what the fuck you say?" I said as I looked up at Nicole in the mirror.

Nicole was silent as I spoke to her, "Shut the fuck up! Jeremy is like a batter on his third strike— he's out of here, and you will not be able to stop me, so, whatever the hell you have planned, erase it because I will take you the fuck out too," I said to her.

"You may be right Nikki, but you cannot stop me from trying. You should know that I am going to try to take you out, so be aware of the woman in the mirror."

"I tell you what bitch. I'll allow you a few moments with your precious Jeremy before I take him out. Will that make you feel better? Will that make you quit talking about all this taking a muther-fucker out and shit?" I asked her just to see if she was serious.

"Yes, Nikki. I would love that so much. Please and thank you," Nicole said.

I thought to myself, *As soon as I kill Jeremy, I'm taking this bitch out the game*. I looked at this weak bitch trading a day in the life of me just to make a few memories with a man that obviously did not want her anymore. She made me so sick with her fucking weakness. I had no idea how in the hell she fell so far off the damn wagon. I pushed thoughts of Nicole to the side and placed my focus back on Jeremy. I was getting excited just at the thought of him seeing my face at his vacation home.

I put the binoculars back to my eyes, and I saw Jeremy again. He was handsome as ever, and his body frame was as lean as ever. Although I could not smell his cologne, I knew he smelled of fresh ocean water in the summer wind's breeze. I looked up and watched as he kissed the woman. Rage and envy enveloped me as I saw her smile at him. The expression on her face was almost like how I would look whenever he looked at me. I looked away, then glanced back. I saw that he was leaving. Not knowing how long he would be gone, I drove away. I knew I had to make my move that night.

I ranted and raved on what to do and how to do it. I had forgotten where I was, so I drove to the park and sat there. Many people came and went, but I knew that I had to be on target when I saw my cheating love for the first time in a year. I sat back in the seat and carefully began to plan. Then, I decided to wait until late night to come back, mainly because then they would be in bed and unaware of any danger lurking nearby.

At eleven P.M., I came back, and the lights were out. I checked my purse to make sure I had my gun, knife and rope. I did, so I parked the car and got out. I noticed the blinds were not down, the windows were up and no screens were attached. I peeped in the window and saw a little boy on the couch; therefore, I pushed the window up more and climbed in. I woke the little boy up and said, "I am your mom's guest, and I need to wake her up. Come show me which room she's in."

He wiped his eyes, and we walked slowly down the hall to their room. I opened the door and turned on the lights. My left hand was over the boy's left shoulder as my right hand stayed on my purse.

Donna woke up and said, "Jeremy, honey, wake up. Baby, please wake up. We have company."

He turned over, and, when he saw his pregnant wife sitting upright in the bed, he looked past her and saw me. As he jumped up, his eyes popped out of his head, and his mouth dropped open.

"Well, hello to you too, Jeremy. You look as if you have seen a ghost. Close your fucking mouth nigga. I'm just a long lost friend that you seemed to have forgotten," I said in a taunting voice.

"Let go of my son, please. I will do anything you ask. Please let him go," Donna said, but I paid her no attention because my eyes were focused on Jeremy and his naked chest.

"Nicole, let him go. He is just a child." Jeremy said in a sweet way.

"Who the hell is Nicole? You killed that bitch a long time ago when you fucked her then told her you didn't want to be with her anymore. I'm here, and my damn name is Nikki. Did you forget about me?" I spoke angrily.

"Ok, Nikki, let him go. I know Nicole is still there, and she is still a good woman," Jeremy replied.

"A good woman my ass. She was weak, and you pushed her over way too many times. That trick is not going to work anymore. Seriously, there is no more Nicole. That bitch died," I said as everyone's eyes focused on me.

I opened my purse with my right hand and threw her some rope. I said, "Gag his mouth and tie him to the bed."

She did not budge, so I reached my right hand in the purse and took out my gun. She gasped as I pointed it to her son's head. I said, "Gag his fucking mouth and tie him to the damn bed, bitch."

With speed, she tied him to the bed. I eased over to Jeremy and touched the ropes to make sure he was secure, and he was. Looking over to her, I said, "Sit in the chair with your feet against the chair legs." She sat there as her son and I walked over to her. I put the boy in her lap as far as he would go and said, "I am going to tie you up, and, if you make a sudden move, it will be nothing for me to kill him. Ask Jeremy. I killed his baby brother with no problem."

"Do what she says, baby," Jeremy mumbled through the gag but I understood him.

Donna sat there and let me gag her mouth, and then tie her feet and arms to the chair. I got the little boy and said, "You can go back to bed. We are playing a game, and it will be over soon."

He yawned and went back to the living room. When the child left, I went over to Jeremy and said, "Do you have any idea how long Nicole has waited for this moment?" He did not say a word. When I walked over to his pregnant wife and pointed the gun at her head, he began trying to run his mouth. I undid the mouth piece just to hear him beg.

"You have me. Leave her out of this. For God's sake, she is pregnant," he pleaded.

"Yeah, she is pregnant with our baby, right? Guess it's a two for one special. Jeremy, I'm sorry. No can do," I said in an evil way.

Donna tried to mumble something, but I walked over to her and slapped the taste out her mouth, twice.

"Bitch, who told you to speak? If I had got what I wanted, your baby would be mine. You don't know what the fuck is going on, so shut the fuck up and let Nicole talk to Jeremy. Fuck it! Go ahead and say what the fuck you have to say," I told Donna as I pulled the gag out of her mouth.

"What do you want from us?" she asked me while crying.

"I don't want a muther-fucking thing from you. I want Jeremy. You stole him from me, and I want him back."

"How did I steal him? He was not yours from the beginning."

"Bitch, if you say that again, I will decapitate your head from your body and then gut your baby from his little head to his penis. Jeremy will always be mine forever. I love him, and you don't," I snapped.

"Just let him go. You can keep me," she pleaded.

"Why in the fuck would I want you? I came all the way from Nevada to get my man. I lost him before because of this muther-fucker named Cowboy," I said as I rubbed my head.

"Don't say anymore," Jeremy spoke out of turn to Donna.

I turned around and looked at him. They locked eyes, and she dropped her head. This bullshit between these two was really beginning to piss me off. I ran up to Donna and sliced her right across the jaw with my knife. She squealed like a fucking pig. I rushed to stuff the gag back into her mouth, and Jeremy tried to break loose as I stuffed the knife back in my purse. I stood there for a few minutes watching the blood rush down her face. Laughing out loud, I said, "Damn, you're bleeding like a hog."

She sobbed as I walked back over to Jeremy and said, "Ok, Nicole. I'm going to get out the way, so you can have your fun with Jeremy. Don't take all muther-fucking day because we have other shit to do."

I reached in my purse and took out the knife. I cut Jeremy's boxers off him, revealing a body that had drove me wild for many nights. I put the knife away and took off my clothes. I looked back at his wife, and she turned her head. I got up and went over to her, leaned her chair back and dragged her closer to the bed, so she could see. "Don't turn your head. Watch Nicole fuck your husband."

I started touching Jeremy, but he did not get hard. I then tasted him but that did not work either, so I leaned over to him and said, "If this dick does not get hard when I taste it again, you will watch me deliver your baby right here, right now."

I placed my mouth back on Jeremy, and he got on hard. I could not help myself because I had always enjoyed pleasing Jeremy. When he was solid hard, I got on top of him and began riding him.

"Oh, how I missed this good dick," Nicole said out loud to cover up the sound of his wife crying. "Tell me it's good to you too Jeremy. Tell me you love me."

He did not say a word until he looked into my face and saw madness, so he replied "I love you Nicole. I love only you."

His body began to tremble as he came. I got off him and tasted what was left in the stalk. I wiped my mouth and laid beside him and rubbed his chest, the way I used to whenever we would finish making passionate love. Riding him that night had made my body come alive, and I knew that it was now or never, but the time was not right. For right then, everything was perfect.

Chapter 17

Laying in the bed with Jeremy felt so good. I tangled my fingers in the locks of hair on his chest. I was happier than I had ever been.

"You awake, Jeremy?" I said as I touched his body over and over.

He mumbled something. Then, I remembered that after I sucked him off, I gagged his mouth again so he couldn't ruin our moment.

"You don't have to say anything because your heart tells the truth, even if your mouth cannot," I said as I enjoyed the feel of his skin beneath my fingers.

I turned my head towards his wife. She was awake and staring at me with such hatred that I began kissing on Jeremy's body just because of the look she had on her face. Seeing that I had her attention, I got on top of him again and began riding him like never before. His body felt the same way it did when we used to make love, a long time ago. His every thrust was perfect as it matched my body's rhythm. I knew he did not want to do it whole heartedly, but he could not deny the way I made him feel whenever I was on top of him. The longer I rode him the more it felt right to have the man I love make love to me and not her. He had no choice. If his dick didn't get hard, then I would have killed his wife and their baby right there. He didn't want that, so he fucked. It would all be over soon.

A few moments later, he started bucking me, and I knew then that his orgasm was complete, but when my orgasm came along, I thumped him harder than I had ever done before. Out of breath and sweaty, I kissed his chest and laid my head upon him. I realized that time must be getting away, and I looked back at the clock on the wall. It read five A.M. I jumped up off my love and said, "Come on, Nikki. You will not keep a hold on me anymore."

"Nicole, don't call me out if you are not prepared to fight it out. I gave you what you've been wanting, and you try this shit again?" I spoke.

"It's over, Nikki. Let it be done with," Nicole said.

"It's not over until I say it's over, dumb bitch." I quickly replied.

Before Nicole could react, I put my hands around her neck and started dragging her backwards. Nicole fell all over the room as I choked her. Jeremy was trying to get up, and Nikki saw him. Nikki said, "Ask him if he loves you or his wife?"

The struggling stopped abruptly, as Nicole walked over to Jeremy and took the rag out of his mouth. She looked into his eyes and asked in a serious manner, "Jeremy, do you love me or her?"

"Nicole, I love you," Jeremy said as he looked away from his wife.

"If you lie to me again, I will do something you don't want me to. Now, I will ask you one last time, and I want the truth. Who do you love— me or her?"

Jeremy looked at me and then his wife and answered, "I love my wife."

"Really?" Nicole said.

"Yes, really. I'm so sorry that I hurt you. I never meant to hurt you. I loved you once, but you became another person. It's like I don't even know you anymore. This was supposed to be our life, but you're letting someone else control you. I can't live like that," he spoke from the heart.

"So, you and I would have had a chance if it wasn't for Nikki," Nicole said.

"Yes. Yes, but now I have found someone to love me, and I love her back. You taught me how to love, and I truly thank you for that. I do love my wife. If I have to die to save her and my son's life, then so be it, but I love my wife," Jeremy said with tears falling down his face.

Nicole fell down at Jeremy's feet and cried. She sobbed and sobbed for all the times in her life she'd loved, and love was unfavorable to her. Jeremy had been her best friend, and she'd had hopes of marrying him, but now he was married to another. Nicole felt that her world was over as she cried more deeply about the man she had loved for a long time. She focused back on Jeremy's face and said, "You don't have any idea how it feels to lose someone, do you? You were my best friend, my soul mate, and you meant the world to me. I never dreamed that I would be here, forcing you to take what I desire to give to you freely. You can have it all with me, can't you see that? My love for you runs deeper than you could ever imagine. Marry me. Let me be the mother of your children. Give me a chance to show you that I can make you just as happy, if not happier," Nicole said as she poured out her heart to Jeremy, while he lay tied up and unfocused on what was being said to him. He looked at me as if he didn't give a fuck about what I was saying. I had seen that look in the past. Jeremy looked at Nicole and closed his eyes.

Nicole continued, "You don't know how it feels to lose everything you had because of what someone else may think, do you? I have loved you for a long time Jeremy, and to know that you got my goods and left me, it did a lot of damage to my soul. I did not think you would have moved on so soon after me, but you did. It makes me think you did not love me at all."

Jeremy still did not look at Nicole but only at his wife.

"Jeremy, I know I was not the best, but I am here to tell you that I can be the one you can love. I have always been there for you, and nothing has ever changed. We have had some good times as well as bad times together, but, somehow, we made it through it all, didn't we? I have made you happy once, and if given the opportunity, I can make you happy again. Do you know how it feels to see love lay helplessly and not be able to do anything to help it?"

Jeremy continued to look at his wife. Nikki saw that he was ignoring Nicole by keeping his eyes locked on the pregnant woman that was tied to the chair.

"Jeremy, do you not hear Nicole fucking talking to you?" I yelled.

"Leave him alone, Nikki. He hears me. He just doesn't understand right now," Nicole said.

"Understand? He will understand if I fuck his wife up," Nikki said.

Jeremy turned and looked at me, full of hatred. In my heart, I truly believed that he was feeding me a bunch of bullshit to keep me from hurting his precious wife, but I was going to show him who was boss. The next time Nicole poured out her heart, he would fucking listen. They were staring at each other like they were in love. She couldn't have him. I refused to let Nicole get hurt again.

I flew off the handle with rage. I took out my knife and stuck it in the top of Donna's stomach. She jerked and screamed through the gag in her mouth. I sliced downwards, opening the top half of Donna's stomach. Jeremy bucked and tried to get up as Donna bit down on the rag from the pain.

Nikki yelled out, "Who do you love? Nicole or your wife?"

He yelled, "Nikki, you fucking bitch. Leave her alone. You can kill me. Leave her the fuck alone, you stupid bitch!"

Nikki looked at him and replied with a laugh "Stupid bitch? What harsh words. Well, I know you don't love Nicole, and she knows you don't love her. I won't ask you the question again. I'm just going to kill you and your wife, bitch."

I took the knife and gutted Donna's stomach all the way open. I reached in, pulled the baby out and dropped that little nigga on the floor. The umbilical cord was still attached so I ripped it out of her body. Blood gushed from her as I picked up the baby and tossed him across the floor and said, "Touchdown." I began laughing and dancing around doing this dance called "My Dougie". The room was filled with nothing but my laughter as Jeremy tried to break free. I looked at him and said, "I told your mother-in-law Rose that I would cut that baby out and drop the breathing child on the floor. There, I kept my promises. Unlike you, I don't lie."

Jeremy started bucking and bucking, but he could not break free. Donna was out cold because the pain was too much for her to comprehend. She sat there, drooped over, and in need of medical care. Nicole slapped me right across the face before I could do any more harm to the baby.

"I told you not to hurt that baby. What the fuck is wrong with you?" Nicole screamed at me as she hit me across the face over and over.

Just at that moment, when Nicole and I became entrenched in our fight, sirens rang out and lights shined through the bedroom curtains. Nicole and I both stop struggling and ran over to the large framed bedroom window that was opened all the way up. Bright lights and police were everywhere, and like a Band-aid on a sore thumb, Nicole saw Dr. John Adams. He was there with the police, trying to take us back to Raymond Neil. *They must think that if he is here, I will turn myself in. What a crock of shit that is,* I thought.

I looked at Nicole.

"Bitch, you snitched on me?" I said to her as we stood there toe to toe.

"Nikki, since you have been in my life, everything has been flipped upside down. All you do is make my life harder. Bitch, you have to go," Nicole said quickly.

"Did you just call me a bitch? Wow! You cursed me," I said to her as I clapped my hands.

Then I heard Dr. Adams speak through the bullhorn, "Nikki, come out, so we can get you some help. I promise I won't let them hurt you."

I yelled back at him from the room, "Fuck you, dick head! Leave me the fuck alone!"

"Nikki, we are here to help you. Nobody is going to get hurt. Come out and please let the hostages go!" Dr. Adams said loudly.

"Why should I trust you? Tell me why?" I said.

"Nikki, you can trust me. Ask Nicole. Tell her, Nicole, that you trust me enough to help you both," Dr. Adams replied.

"Nikki, this is the police. We have the house surrounded. We will shoot to kill if you do not stand down and let the hostages go," a policeman yelled out.

"I'll let them go when you go to hell," I screamed back at the man.

I observed Jeremy and saw he was not paying attention to us. He seemed to be lost in thought. With my gun still drawn, I looked at him and asked with sincerity, "Did you ever love me, or did you just play with my emotions? I just think that, if you love someone like you are supposed to, you don't get over them as quick as you did me," I asked in need of a response from Jeremy.

Jeremy turned his head towards me and let out a small laugh. He then whispered, "Love is an understatement, and to hear you speak so casually about it, I just had to laugh a little. Nicole, I will be honest with you. In spite of everything we had been through, I loved you once in my life, but that time is long gone. I have moved on, and I love Donna. You will always have a part in my life, but it is Donna I love now. She has my heart, and she is my soul mate. No matter what you do to me, you can't make me love you as you want me to. You were a wonderful friend, but I needed more, and Donna filled the spot. I know you do not understand, but one day, you will. At least I hope you understand one day," he concluded.

Nicole cried and cried as he spoke. Dr. Adams and the police negotiator called out for Nicole, but no answer was heard. Nicole had truly put her heart in her hand, and no words could explain how hurt she was feeling. After glancing at Jeremy, the baby on the floor, and Donna, Nicole looked up and said "Lord, Forgive me for Nikki's sins."

Nicole walked closer to Jeremy, and Nikki said, "What are you doing?"

"Something you said I would not ever have the strength to do. By the looks of everything around me, I have found the strength you did not think existed," Nicole spoke to me with hurt in her voice.

"Bitch, get out the way. You are confused and lost," I said to Nicole.

"I am a long way from being confused. I admit I used to be, but no more. I have you to thank for that," Nicole replied.

Leaning toward Jeremy, I said, "I'm about to let you go. If you make a false move when I untie you, your ass is grass, and I will be the lawnmower that will mow your ass down."

He nodded and slowly I untied him. Jeremy and I stared at each other eye to eye. Then, he looked over at his wife still slumped over in the chair. She appeared to be dead.

"Go over to your wife, Jeremy, and talk to her," Nicole said to Jeremy as if I was not there.

"You act like I am not standing here with the gun, Nicole," I said to her, but Jeremy was over at his wife's body in a few short strides.

He felt her wrist for a pulse. Then, he felt her neck for a pulse. He even put his head to her chest to see if he could hear some form of light breathing. He did not say if he found a pulse or not, and he would not look at me. He touched her face and whispered, "I am so sorry I got you involved in this. I love you so much, Donna. Don't ever let what happened here prevent you from trusting anyone else again. Chances are I may not make it, but I pray you remember how much I truly love you, and only you."

He touched her hand once more and let out tears on the bent fingers that were under his nose. Jeremy cried like a new born baby fresh out the womb for the pain he was going through. At first, I felt kind of bad about the shit.

He looked back at me and asked, "Can I pick him up, please?"

"Yes, Jeremy. Pick up your son," Nicole replied.

He kneeled down on one knee and picked up the new born baby. Jeremy touched the bottom of his feet. The sudden movement of the child caused Jeremy to jump. He quickly turned his eyes towards me and then focused back on the baby. He then, started talking to the child.

"Little man, I love you and it means the world to me that you were a fighter. Your mom wanted to name you after me, but to me, you deserve a name much greater than mine."

He kissed his son on the forehead. He then wrapped the child in the mother's nearby robe and placed him back on the floor where he was. Not able to hold in his words, he began talking as if his life depended on it, and in a sense it did.

"If you love me as you say you do, then why hurt my wife and child? Why did you have to kill them? Do what you want to me but hurt them no more. It is me that you believed to have caused you so much unbearable pain in your life. They, like many others, are not to blame for the experiences that you went gone through. I ask you to please not hurt them anymore."

"Touché. Touché, Jeremy. What a grand speech you just made. What brought that along?" I asked him in a teasing voice.

"The truth is what brought this on. You know Nicole, I loved you, and I had no idea why I broke it off with you until now," Jeremy said as he kept his eyes on me.

"What do you mean, 'until now'?" I asked because I was sure Nicole needed to know.

"A part of me felt that you were incapable of loving anyone other than yourself. You would never let me in, as much as I tried to fit in. You kept me at a distance, and you never made me feel like you needed me as much as I needed you. I always had to reach for you, but you would pull further away. Then, one day, I woke up and a thought came to me that I could not continue to play charades with you. That was the day I asked you if you could be completely honest with me, and you replied no because you only had yourself and no one else. Nicole, that was the day I had to let you go. Now looking back, I do see that you are a fucking mad woman that is selfish and impossible of loving someone like me," Jeremy spoke with sadness and hurt in his voice.

"You selfish bitch, are you fucking kidding me? I loved you and would have given you the world, but you wanted to be with other women," I screamed.

"I only fucked those other women to make you mad!" he yelled out.

"You did a damn good job, but I'm not mad. I'm fucking pissed off. And see where your games got you today?" I retorted.

"Yes I do, and I hate you for fucking up my world," he said, while staring me right in the face.

"Walk bitch," was the only response I could manage because I knew Nicole wanted to go on and on, but I, on the other hand, could not have cared less for it.

Jeremy lifted up his hands and started walking towards the door. Right before he got close to the door, he said, "Nicole, how could you be so ruthless, heartless and so evil? You never used to be that way."

Jeremy looked back over his shoulder at me with eyes full of anger.

Laughing my vindictive laugh, I replied, "Nicole isn't heartless, ruthless and evil. She's a good girl. This bitch you see right here? Oh, I'm the muther-fucker," I pointed my gun back at him and continued, "So get to stepping, bitch. After I kill you, then I'm going to kill Nicole. Fuck the both of you, weak bitches."

Click, click, click. My muther-fucking head banged and banged like a drummer. *Bang. Bang*. It seemed like my brain was trying to jump out of my head.

"Nikki, he is already hurt. You have made your point. He is in pain, and the pain of losing a child is pain enough," I heard Nicole say.

"I guess you want me to let the bastard go?" I said as Jeremy interrupted us.

"Nicole, please tell her to let me go. Please tell her to let me go," Jeremy begged.

"I have this pain in my head. Stop it, Nicole. You will not win. He deserves to die. Let this pussy-ass dog die," I said to Nicole as she forced the pain to almost overtake me.

"Nikki, let him go. Just let him go," Nicole began pleading with me.

"I thought we were in this together?" I asked Nicole.

"Nikki, we are in this together, and nothing can stop that, but think of all we have done to get here."

Nicole pleaded with me in such a way that I actually began thinking. I had to think because this pain in my head was unbearable.

"Don't you think it should end here?" Nicole asked me.

"Hell yeah, the shit *is* going to end here tonight, believe it or not. It may not end the way you want it to, but it will end, all the same," I replied.

Jeremy stopped walking and began listening to us debate, but I pushed the gun in his back and spoke, "Keep on walking and please do not stop again."

He started back walking, but at a slower pace than before.

"Nikki, I am warning you. Let him go, and let him go now," Nicole said.

We got to the front door and I said, "Stop here."

We stopped at the front door, and I said, "Whoa! Are you trying to go for bad, Nicole? Having a few stolen moments with him has changed your mind?"

"Nikki, I don't want anything to happen to Jeremy. Let us end this."

I looked over at her and said, "Maybe. Maybe not. Just keep walking."

We made it to the living room, and I noticed the little boy was gone. That little muther-fucker was the one who had called for help. I should have taken him the fuck out.

"Thank you Nicole. You let that little bastard get away. You could have had more time with Jeremy, but you kept fucking with my head!" I yelled at her. "The little bastard got help. That is the fucking reason why these damn pigs are here. They even brought along the big pig in the blanket, Dr. Adams."

She did not speak. Usually when she did not speak that meant she was plotting on something. Her plotting always ended with me showing her who was boss and who was not.

"Open the door very slowly and please remember, I do have a gun full of bullets, ready to wax your ass, and I will shoot the fuck out of you,"

When we appeared at the door, Dr. Adams said, "Nikki, settle down, and let us help you."

"Wow, someone finally called me by my name and not Nicole's. These bitches act like they can't tell us apart," I said. I could barely see because the lights were bright, and if it was not for Jeremy's tall shadow, I would have been blind.

"Nikki, lower the gun and release him. You will get the best care. No one here wants to see you hurt. What do you say?" Dr. Adams asked.

"I say go to hell, I don't need help. What the fuck is wrong with you?" I asked.

"Nikki, if you don't turn yourself in, they will shoot you. And none of these policemen want to hurt you," Dr. Adams said as I continued to stand behind Jeremy.

"Nicole, don't let Nikki make up your mind. It is your life too. Nicole, you have the right to be a part of it. Be a part of the decision that Nikki wants to make for you both. Don't let her continue to dominate your life," Dr. Adams said.

"Shut up. Shut the fuck up. I exist because Nicole is too weak to handle the challenges that are in her life. She can't hack it. So, doctor, you have me to talk to, and if you call on her again, I will kill them both," I said loud and clear.

I wondered, *How in the hell did they get Dr. Adams all the way down here from Nevada?* These muther-fuckers must have been following me. Or then again, they might have been following Jeremy. Who gives a fuck? I wondered if they knew about all those other fuckers I'd killed. Well, it didn't matter now. Fuck them all.

I then, kicked Jeremy in the back, and he fell to his knees, fully exposing me to the people surrounding us. I could feel Nicole, trying to break loose in me, but I spoke to her as I looked around at everything.

"Nicole you don't want to do what you are thinking. Cut that foolish thought out."

"Nikki, you have no idea just what I am thinking," Nicole said to me in a confident tone of voice that made my eyes squint.

Out of nowhere, I began to feel pain running rapidly through my body like never before. I shook my head and knew that bitch Nicole was trying to come forth. She was getting stronger with each passing minute, but I couldn't let her win. I had come too far and had done too much just to let Nicole fuck it up. The more pain she gave me, the weaker I became, but she didn't need to know that. I shook my head to shake it off because killing Jeremy was the reason I'd come this far.

Looking at Jeremy's back made me feel angry.

"I don't see what Nicole sees in you," I spat.

"Nikki, drop the gun," I heard the policeman yell through the bullhorn.

I looked over at him and dropped the gun. Then, I pulled the knife out of my back and placed it to Jeremy's throat.

"Drop the knife, Nikki, or we will shoot," I heard a policeman say.

I saw a tear roll down Jeremy's cheek, and I heard him say "I forgot to tell you that I am sorry for ever hurting you, Nicole. Forgive me," he spoke with sincerity.

I leaned down and kissed him on the cheek that held his tear and said, "Forgive this."

I cut his throat from left to right. However, I never counted on the police shooting me multiple times. The knife fell out of my hands as my body fell backwards. I lay there staring at the sky and watching my life flash before my eyes. I saw Jeremy, Marvin, and my father. My mind replayed all the hurtful things they'd done to me.

A man came into my view as I was looking up. He was Marvin, but how so when I'd killed him? I frowned, and my heart began to beat normally again. He placed his head to my chest, but before he could move back, I reached up and locked my teeth into his neck. I grabbed his head with my hands, and gritted and gritted until I pulled a huge chunk out of his neck. I lay back down with his bloody veins and skin tangled in my mouth. Marvin screamed as he fell over, and I smiled and thought that, *If you weren't dead then, bitch, you dead now*.

Reality was, I bit this huge-ass plug of meat out of a police officers' neck. He was stupid enough to bend down to see if I was breathing. Damn, I thought he was Marvin. I wanted to kill that bitch all over again. I looked over at Jeremy and closed my eyes.

Epilogue

As we walked inside the small room for group therapy, a patient said, "Come on, Doc. Finish that story you were telling us. I'm so anxious to hear about Nikki and Jeremy."

"Tonya, go on and sit down. You're going to forget after I tell you," Dr. Webb-Adams joked.

Other patients laughed, as we all sat down for group therapy. Dr. Webb-Adams placed her small framed glasses on her head and looked out into the crowd of women and asked, "Are you all ready?"

"Yo Doc! So where is this patient now that killed all those people?" the patient asked.

"Now, you know I cannot answer that. It's doctor-patient confidentiality. You know that. I would never share your secrets either," she explained. "Though these doctors tell you that the story is just a myth. Here at St. Elizabeth's in Washington, D.C., don't believe the hype. Hospital names have been changed by now as well as her real name. I knew her personally before and after she broke out."

"See, that's why we fuck with you Doc, 'cause you cool and not all stuck up like these other doctors in here," the patient suffering from immediate short term amnesia and memory loss started to explain before forgetting what she was talking about.

"Stop lying, Doc. You didn't know that girl," another patient blurted out.

"Of course, she does. She said Nikki was her twin sister."

"Fuck naw Doc. Your twin sister? I don't believe that. If so, then what happened to her after she killed Jeremy and got all shot up? If she is real, it's no fucking way she killed all those people and is still alive. That bitch was a fucking loony tune," the nonbeliever from the group said.

"Come on doc. You said you would never lie to us," a patient said with tears.

"Why are you about to cry? She said Nikki was truly her twin sister," another patient said.

"Get the fuck out of here," the patient with memory loss spoke.

"I'm so for real. They have her housed here," Dr. Webb-Adams spoke out.

"It's kind of funny actually. Can you all keep a secret?" Dr. Webb-Adams continued as she leaned in for effect, knowing damn well they wouldn't remember this shit she was telling them after group therapy was over. And even, if they did, nobody in there would believe a bunch of fucking whackos!

"Yes," they all answered in unison, excited that someone took the time to share a real story with them that was actually interesting, instead of the usual boring and depressing bullshit.

"We have the same last name. Her name was Nikki Webb," Dr. Webb-Adams said looking around at the patients; but none of them caught on except for the smart bitch that questioned everything like she was a fucking secret agent.

"Security!" she screamed as she got up to run and call for help, but I had already pounced on that ass.

"Bring the meds!" I yelled louder than her as I muffled her screams.

Security grabbed her up, while the nurse stuck the syringe in her arm. She was a determined little bitch too, and I liked it. It reminded me of myself back in my hay day. She kept trying to tell them that it was me, but by the time she got it out, she was already subdued. I dispersed the rest of the group to their nurses and texted my husband to let him know that I would be home late. After he didn't respond to my text quickly enough, I decided to call.

"Hey, Mr. Adams," I cooed over the phone to the man who'd saved my life, as I rolled my eyes at the thought of how long I'd have to play nice.

"I just saw your text, and we will be waiting when you get here. Both the twins are napping, so it will be just you and me if you don't take too long," he said while cheesing through the phone. I was getting sick by the second just thinking about what he was implying.

"Kiss Jeremiah and Jerrica for me. I have to make a stop before I get there." That was all I said before I ended the phone call.

I walked towards the smart mouthed bitch's room and looked through the glass window. I'd played nice for long enough, and it had been killing me. Now Nikki was ready to make a grand appearance, and I knew just who I would start with....

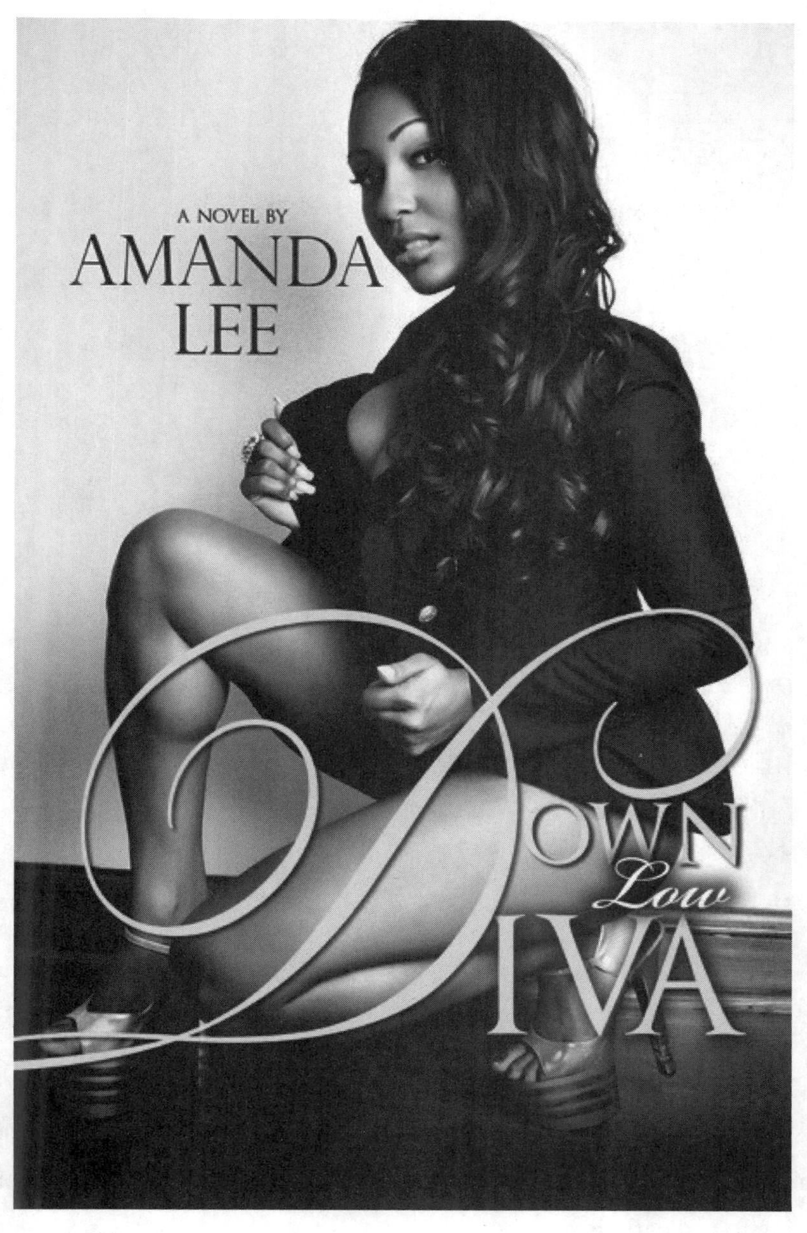

Now Available

A Novel By

AMANDA
LEE

Sneak Peak

School girls and regular house wives go to bed early while bitches like me stay up and ready to fuck. We can't go to bed doing only do the missionary position or regular doggy style, freaks like me need more and going to bed early is not it.

I opened up my luggage and thought about what to wear for Peter. I brought along a few new wardrobes but I needed something that says "Spank me I've been a bad kitty." Over to my right above the nurse uniform was nice but, there was, the two piece cat outfit. Thinking how "I almost forgot about that one because when I saw the pleasure getter it screamed I bite." Getting in front of the mirror I rubbed my body down with strawberry motion lotion. Carefully I parted my hair down the middle and tied a ball on each side. Glancing back to the mirror I had to make sure they were even and they were. Placing my cat ears on my head I with ease drew cat whiskers on my face with eye liner and smothered my lips with red lipstick, taking a napkin I kissed it to remove the excess.

After putting on my cat face the top was a natural because the only part covered was the nipples. Noticing my bald pussy I put on the candy and continued to admire my own firm and plump breast. They looked dam good and I just had to rub them and give them a slight squeeze. Touching of my own self caused mere pleasure come out of my mouth. Thinking seductively "I need to save this for Peter" but the thought of touching my pussy made me question "Why not fuck yourself? You look good enough to lick clean." Anyway Peter was taking too long and the decision became anonymous to be my own meal. I lay across the bed, closed my eyes and started caressing my breast. Half way through the breast touching I heard a knock at the door. Glancing at the clock on the wall, I knew it had to be Peter and if it wasn't whoever it was, they were fucking me.

I looked over at the table and had to making sure I had hand cuffs, silk bandanas, whip cream, rope and yes eatable lotion, the key ingredients to rock a world. Thinking about Peter's cock I looked at the three thick dildo's on the table and thought "Just in case he goes limp tonight, he can choose the one he wants to use on me" Getting up off the bed and liking the setting on the table I had to make sure my whip was ready; therefore, I smacked it in the air. My eyes increased when I heard the cracking sound for it made me shiver and reminded me why I like fucking Peter. He has eight stout inches and a mushroom cap to make me run for the hills. His pure beef stick would bang me out of control and often times he has my sexy ass hollering.

After all this licking and eating ass I needed a down home fucking and if Peter brings it like he usually does, I will not be disappointed. Not to keep my good dick waiting I went to the door. Just like Peaches said he would, it was Peter but I already knew who it was so I turned the lights off and opened the door.

TO BE CONTINUED…

Author Amanda Lee

www.authoramandalee.com

www.facebook.com/authoramandalee

www.twitter.com/diamez22

4 PLAY...

Never Say Never

NOW AVAILABLE

www.amazon.com
www.tljbookstore.com

Get ready to go on the ride of your life with Felix and his 4 women of choice. Nikki, Rhonda, Meka, and Toya each have a thing for Felix that they cannot describe. It's not only because he is the youngest and most sought after attorney in Washington, DC or the fact that he is handling a high profile multi-million dollar divorce case, but that he serves them real well! Felix makes it happen with each woman like they are each his woman, and that's just what they expect from him...A monogamous relationship which is what they each think they are getting. What will happen when jealousy, lies, deceit, millions of dollars, paternity, and feelings become at risk? Is 4play enough to make Felix fall in love? Do you think Felix will keep getting over or will the women get even? Ride the roller coaster as he vows to never fall in love but is enjoying the "loving" from 4 women from 4 different walks of life. You will definitely be able to relate to one of these women if not all! Laugh, cry, and enjoy Felix's lavish lifestyle of 4play!!!!

The Wrong He's Done
A Novel by
Nathan Gadsden

Greatness is only a step away for Damon Masters. Partnership at his firm is within his grasp; all Damon has to do is prove to the firm that he can handle its main client. His wife, Priscilla, has found entreprenuerial success at her boutiques. The only speed bump in life is his annoying mother-in-law, Queen, whose jealous ways wreak havoc on his marriage. When the firms client turns out to be Frank Vanetti, mob boss and racketeer, Damon has to decide whether his life is worth risking for the idea of greatness. In the meantime, Queen has managed to split his household, leaving him to pick up the pieces of his fractured marriage. With the help of his best friend, Antoine, Damon goes on a road trip to meet past loves and reevaluate where life went wrong. But walking away from Vanetti does not mean that Damon is safe from the mob. And best friend Antoine's schemes and manipulations seek to sabotage Damon's trip and further destroy what is left of his marriage. When ex-loves remind Damon of what he had, and all the drama and chaos of his current life become overwhelming, he must decide whether his current life is worth fighting for.

NOW AVAILABLE

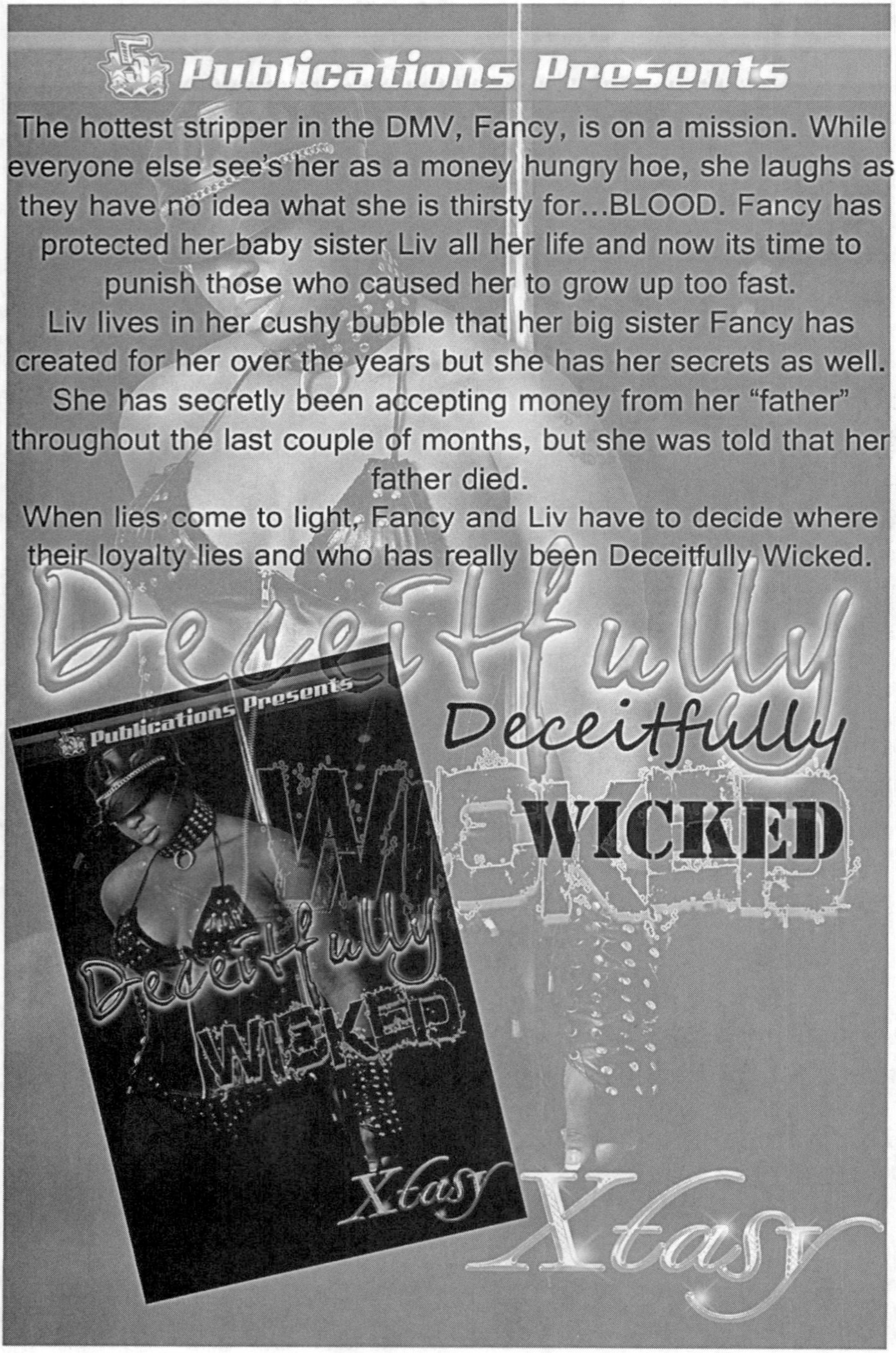

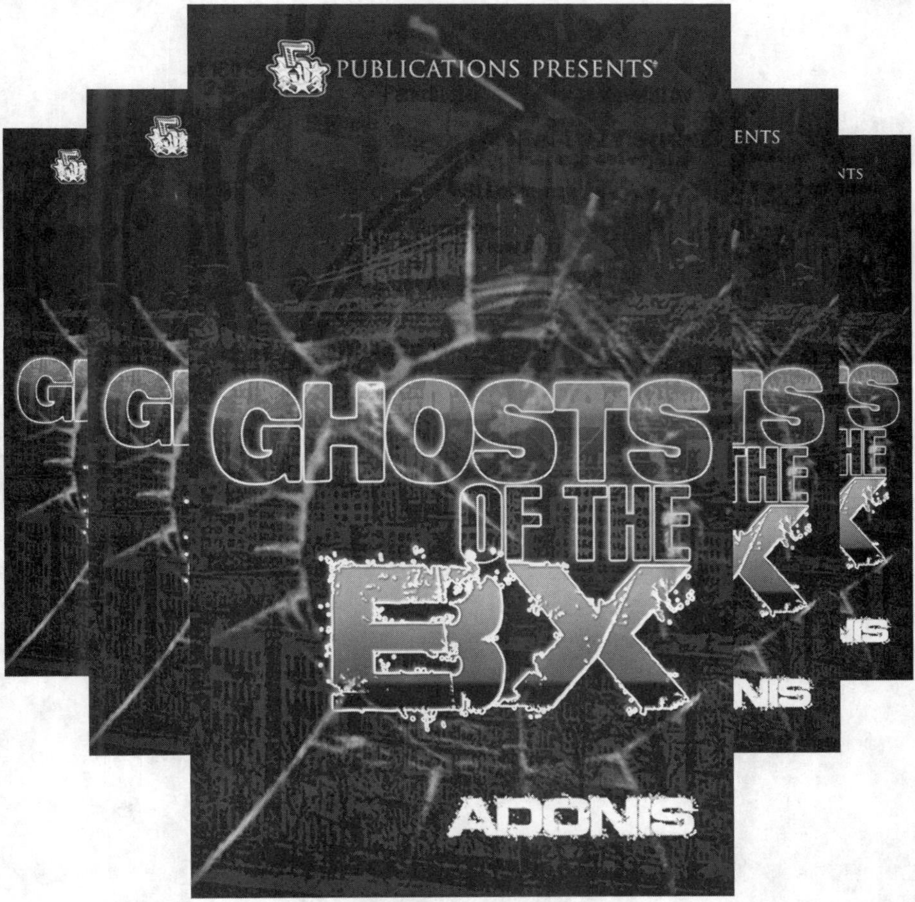

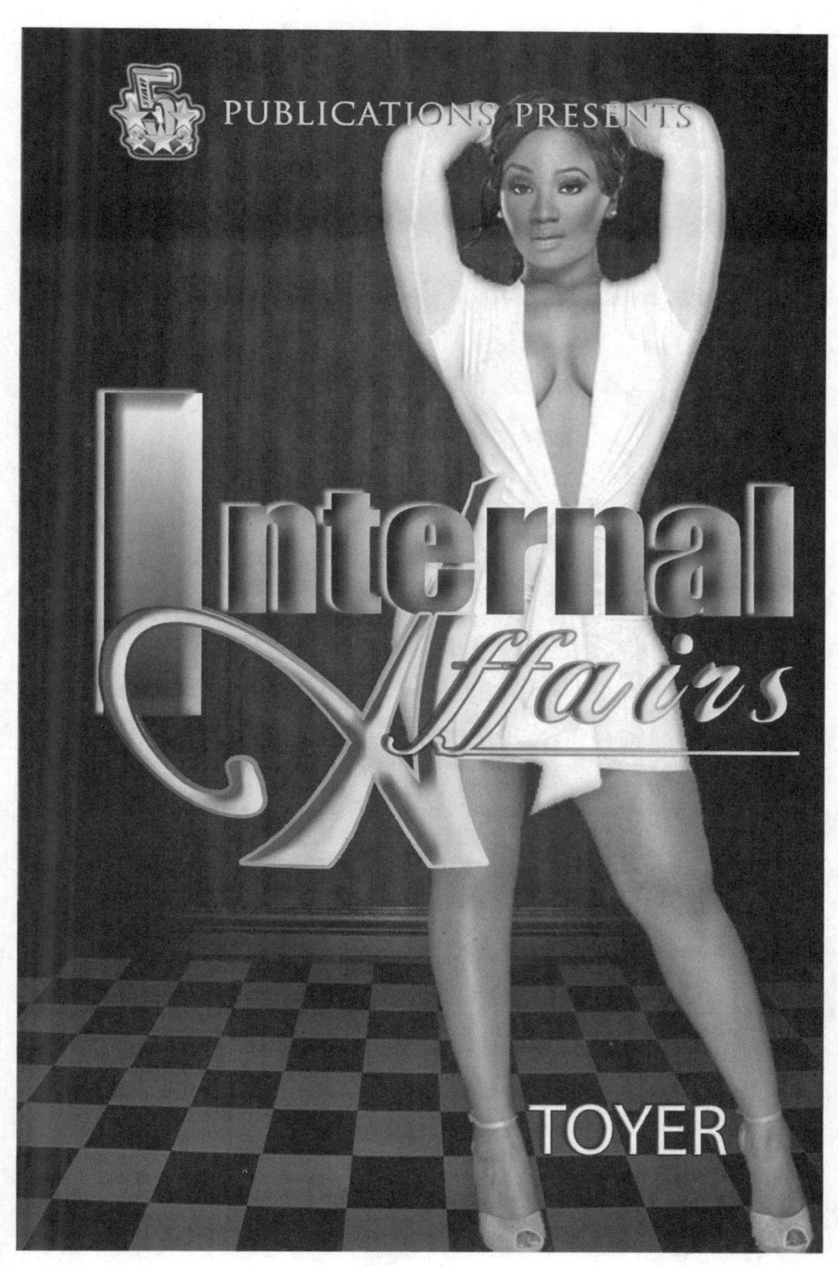

COMING SUMMER 2012

COMING FALL 2012